Reycraft Books
55 Fifth Avenue
New York, NY 10003
Reycraftbooks.com

Reycraft Books is a trade imprint and trademark of Newmark Learning, LLC.

Text © 2022 Salima Alikhan

All rights reserved. No portion of this book may be reproduced, stored in a retrieval system, or transmitted in any form or by any means, electronic, mechanical, photocopying, recording, or otherwise, without written permission from the publisher. For information regarding permission, please contact info@reycraftbooks.com.

Educators and Librarians: Our books may be purchased in bulk for promotional, educational, or business use. Please contact sales@reycraftbooks.com.

This is a work of fiction. Names, characters, places, dialogue, and incidents described either are the product of the author's imagination or are used fictitiously. Any resemblance to actual persons, living or dead, is entirely coincidental.

Sale of this book without a front cover or jacket may be unauthorized. If this book is coverless, it may have been reported to the publisher as "unsold or destroyed" and may have deprived the author and publisher of payment.

Library of Congress Control Number: 2022903721

ISBN: 978-1-4788-7454-6

Photo Credits:
Pages 3,23,33,43,61,83,105,117,135,151: Tetiana Lazunova/Getty Images
Author photo: Sam Bond Photography
Illustrator photos courtesy of Atieh Sohrabi and W. J. Naalchigar

Printed in Dongguan, China. 8557/0522/19134
10 9 8 7 6 5 4 3 2 1

First Edition Hardcover published by Reycraft Books 2022.

Reycraft Books and Newmark Learning, LLC, support diversity and the First Amendment, and celebrate the right to read.

To all my students. — S.A.

Soraya & the Yeti

by Salima Alikhan

illustrated by Atieh Sohrabi

"Basil Goes to Panama"
illustrated by Jennifer Naalchigar

contents

1	A Crystal Kingdom	3
2	The Face in the Mountain	23
3	Discovery	33
4	Basil	43
5	Mount Bergen	61
6	The Hunt	82
7	Punished	105
8	The Last-Minute Prop	117
9	A Poet's Request	135
10	A Confession	151
	Magic Adventures Comic: "Basil Goes to Panama"	167

A Crystal Kingdom

Nimbla Moony's magic gripper boots pierced the ice as she scaled the highest peak on the snow-planet Arborg. In the distance, ice palaces built on great floating icebergs soared into the blizzardy sky. At the very top of the mountain, a little lost Snarfdrizzle clung to a crag, terrified. It had about two minutes before it would freeze to death.

"Hold tight, little Snarfdrizzle—I'm coming!" said Nimbla, as giant snowflakes the size of dinner plates whizzed past her head.

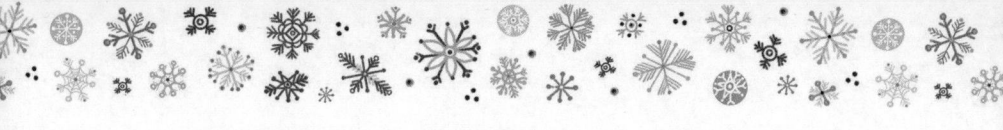

Soraya looked up from the page she was reading and peeked outside the school bus window at a snowy world as white as Arborg. Then she slipped her new comic, *Nimbla Moony and the Snarfdrizzle*, back into her pocket.

Nimbla Moony, Soraya's favorite comic book heroine, had done just about every daring thing in the universe. But even Soraya had to admit that Nimbla had never visited a ski lodge as cool as the one sitting on the hill in front of her school bus.

"It's like a crystal kingdom," her friend Christoff whispered, pressing his nose to the cold bus window.

It *was* like a crystal kingdom. Little frost crystals laced the sides of the windowpane, framing the world outside the bus like a Christmas card. It looked as if they were at the top of the world. Soraya imagined a glittering ice castle somewhere up there and all sorts of ice-fairy creatures with veils of dusty snow.

"The snow must be at least four feet deep," said Soraya's friend Naomi. "You two should stop sticking your noses right up to the window. They could freeze to the glass."

Bold white mountains rose all around them. The school bus wheezed up the endless driveway of the Alpine Ski Lodge, which stood on a slope below Mount Bergen. To Soraya, Mount Bergen might as well have been Mount Everest—it rose impossibly high, its snowy peak lost in the clouds.

Both fourth-grade classes at Soraya's elementary school were going to the lodge for a weekend ski trip. The lodge looked cozy and inviting. It was a big, three-story wooden building with warm yellow windows and smoke pouring out of the chimneys.

"This is even cooler than Balabrook Caverns," Christoff said.

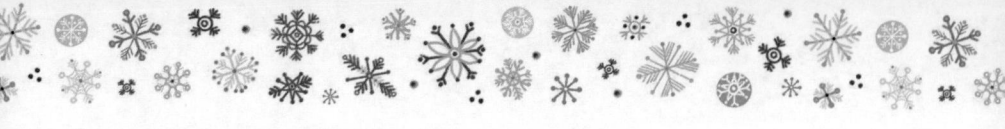

Soraya privately agreed, but she didn't want to say anything bad about the caverns. That was where the class had gone on their last field trip, and where Soraya and her new friends Christoff and Naomi had rescued a sweet dragon named Humphrey. They'd discovered him in a hidden chamber of the caverns and helped reunite him with his family.

Soraya pinched herself to make sure it was all real. Friends. That word still felt weird. Making friends was a new thing for Soraya. She wasn't the best at it. It still felt odd that Christoff and Naomi *wanted* to hang out with her.

"Why are you pinching yourself?" Naomi asked her. "Doesn't that hurt?"

"No reason," said Soraya.

Christoff stared thoughtfully at the lodge. "You know," he said, "if it wasn't so cheerful, that lodge looks like it could be haunted. Aren't ski lodges always haunted?"

"It's definitely not haunted."

Soraya's mom popped her head up from the seat behind them. As the bus slowed down, she started collecting luggage.

"The PTA worked so hard to raise money for this trip," she said. "We wouldn't have booked a haunted lodge." She made a stern face. "Not that there even is such a thing, Soraya."

Soraya bent to pick up her suitcase, trying to hide her scowl. The only un-fun thing about this trip was that her mom was one of the chaperones. In Soraya's opinion, this was completely unnecessary. Didn't they have enough adults already?

In addition to Soraya's mom, there were the two fourth-grade teachers, Ms. Staples and Mr. Haroyan, and four parent chaperones. But when Soraya's mom heard that the classes had been given permission to rehearse their play, *The Snow Queen*, on the lodge's stage, she had volunteered to come too.

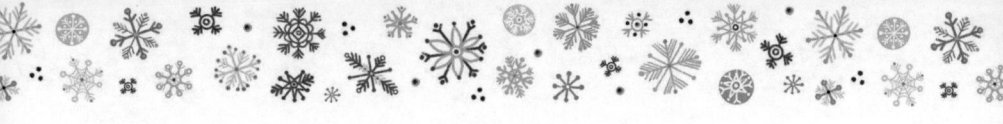

It was the weirdest thing. Soraya hadn't even realized her mom had ever heard of *The Snow Queen*. Her mom was an accountant who liked numbers and wore beige. The only time she'd ever seen her mom use her imagination was when she was deciding what color pen to buy.

When Soraya had first found out her mom was coming on the trip, she'd said, "Mom, are you sure you want to do this? I'm sure it'll be noisy and messy."

"I know," her mom had said brightly. "It will be fun. Since the lodge owners have agreed to let us use their stage, we'll do a dress rehearsal there for the guests! Plus, it'll be a chance for you and me to bond."

"But I'm not even *in* the play," Soraya reminded her mom. "I hate being on stage."

"I know," her mom said, her shoulders drooping a little. "But we'll be at the lodge together, at least."

Soraya squirmed with guilt. In truth, she wanted as much time as possible away from her mom that weekend. She wanted to curl up next to the big fireplace in the lodge (she assumed the lodge had a big fireplace) so she could keep working on drawing and writing her own comic books. She'd been doing a lot of that lately. Right now, her comics and sketchbook were hidden at the very bottom of her bag because her mom didn't exactly approve of Soraya spending time reading comics, much less making her own. Soraya's mom considered comic books a waste of time compared with schoolwork.

"Comics are all well and good, Soraya," her mom would say. "But paying attention to schoolwork is how you'll *really* have a successful future."

Which was why Soraya was looking forward to sneaking off to draw and write while her mom was busy with the play.

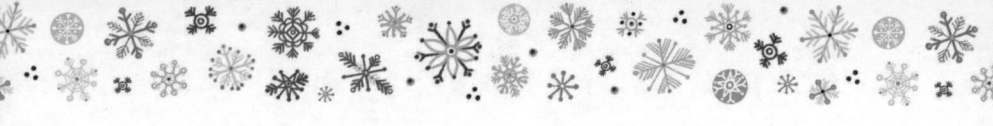

Soraya frowned. If her mom weren't there, she wouldn't have to hide at all.

The bus parked. Students, teachers, and chaperones stood up as everyone gathered their luggage.

"You two can still be in the play if you want," Soraya murmured to Christoff and Naomi as they struggled off the bus with their bags. Both of her friends had decided not to be in the play when she'd told them she wasn't going to be. "You don't have to skip it just because of me."

"I don't like being on stage anyway," said Naomi, which was true.

"I don't either," said Christoff, which was not true. He loved performing. "I'm looking forward to skiing and exploring instead."

Soraya felt like pinching herself again. How had she ended up with friends who wanted to hang out with *her* instead of doing other fun things?

The class scrambled off the bus and onto the driveway of the lodge, which had been plowed. They stared at the grounds, ooh-ing and ahh-ing. There were several buildings on the property, some of them across a big field from the lodge. Soraya could see the ski lift on the lawn. Gondolas were taking skiers up the mountain. People's ski clothes were bright spots of color against all the white. On the other side of the big lawn, right in front of the lodge, was a steep snowy cliffside.

"I keep expecting to see Santa here," said Christoff, grinning.

"Or a stable for his reindeer," said Naomi. She pointed. "That snow is perfect for skiing."

Soraya wasn't looking forward to skiing as much as she was to hunkering down by the fire with hot chocolate and her comics, but she didn't say so. Plus, after refusing to be in the play, she figured she owed her friends some time skiing. She might even like it.

Nimbla Moony comic books always made skiing look easy—though, of course, Nimbla used hover-skis, which worked on any surface.

"Let's go in," said Christoff, heading toward the lodge.

The lobby of Alpine Lodge was everything Soraya hoped it would be: high ceilings with wooden beams, a gigantic stone fireplace with a flickering fire, lots of comfy-looking chairs and rugs, and a table set out with cookies, tea, and hot chocolate.

"We can get some of that later." Christoff tugged at Soraya, who stared longingly at the fire. "Let's explore outside first."

Soraya's mom bustled up behind them, her cheeks pink with cold. "It is lovely, isn't it?"

They walked past the shop in the lobby where guests rented ski boots and skis, and checked in with the front desk clerk.

"Everyone with rooms on the second floor, come with me," Soraya's mom called.

Naomi, Christoff, Soraya, and a bunch of other students followed Soraya's mom out of the lobby and up the wide, purple-carpeted staircase. Electric candles flickered in brackets on the walls. Big portraits of imposing-looking people hung from the wall on the landing.

"I think their eyes are following me," said Christoff.

Soraya's mom hustled them to the second floor and down a long hallway.

"There must be more than a hundred rooms in this building!" Naomi exclaimed. "I can't believe this is just one hall."

"What's that?" Soraya pointed at a large metal plate with a handle on it that was built right into the wall.

"Oh," said her mom. "That looks like an old-fashioned laundry chute. I bet every floor

has one. You pull the handle to open the door to the chute. Hotel workers can toss sheets and towels into it, and they fall down and land in a bin in the laundry room."

"Cool," said Christoff.

"Here's your room, girls." Soraya's mom showed Naomi and Soraya into a room at the end of the hall, with yellow wallpaper and two beds. "Christoff, you're across the hall. I think Derek is your roommate."

"I know," Christoff said with a sigh. "Derek snores."

"I need to help the other kids find their rooms," Soraya's mom said. "Then I'm going downstairs to check the stage and make sure it's ready for us." She hurried off down the hall to help the other students.

Soraya went to the window of her and Naomi's room. The world looked like a winter wonderland from here.

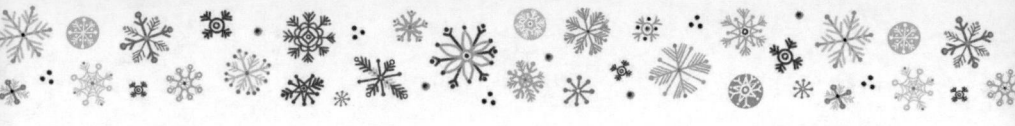

It was the perfect setting for a comic book adventure. Her fingers itched to get back to her sketchbook.

"Let's put on warm clothes and get outside," said Naomi, who was already pawing through her suitcase.

"Okay," said Christoff, still glum. "But I'm warning you, if Derek snores too loud tonight, I'm either sleeping in the hallway or on the floor in your room."

He left to go change.

While Naomi zipped up an extra sweater and pulled on her elegant green coat, Soraya tried to get her coat out of her bag. She had taken it off in the warm hotel lobby and stuffed it into her suitcase. It was so puffy that she'd had to wedge it in tightly. But she loved her new coat, which she had picked out especially for this trip. Her excitement was

enough to distract her for a moment from her mom's weirdness about the play.

As soon as Soraya's parka popped out of the suitcase, it puffed up.

Naomi started to giggle. "You weren't kidding when you said your coat reminds you of a space suit."

Soraya had to laugh, too. She struggled into her coat and stood in front of the mirror. The coat was iridescent, with pillowy little sections that looked like bubbles.

"It's like Nimbla Moony's bubble cape," she said proudly. "Or as much like a bubble cape as a parka can be."

"It's amazing!" Naomi said. "Mine feels boring now."

"Yours is perfect," said Soraya. Naomi's was sleek and efficient, exactly the kind of warm coat Naomi would have.

Out in the hallway, Christoff waited for them in his bright orange coat with a sewed-on penguin patch.

They waddled down the hall, past the two Katies in their pink and purple parkas. Both Katies were in Soraya's class, and one of them was actually named Madison. But they looked and acted so much alike that Soraya called them Katie and Katie 2.0. They always wore pink or purple, always had shiny hair, and always made fun of Soraya.

"Nice coat, Soraya," said Katie 2.0 with a smirk.

"At least *my* parka will protect me if I fall," Soraya retorted, patting her puffy coat. "You won't be so lucky."

They went down the stairs and into the lobby, where many other kids from their classes stood, bundled up in their own winter gear. Soraya was pleased that none of their coats were as space-like as hers.

"Class, I want everyone to stick close together," Ms. Staples said. "We're not leaving the grounds today, but there's plenty to do right out in the yard. We'll head back inside around five-thirty for dinner. Let's go!"

The class practically crawled over each other to get out of the doors. They raced off, slipping and sliding, into the snow.

"Lopsided snow angel," cried Christoff, falling back into the snow and waving his arms and legs.

"You are so *weird*," said Katie.

One nice thing about being friends with Christoff and Naomi was that now the Katies called all three of them weird, instead of just Soraya. Christoff and Naomi cared a lot less about being called weird, though. Soraya secretly did care, and wished she didn't.

The snow crunched under Soraya's boots. Several kids ran by her. Within seconds, a snowball fight broke out.

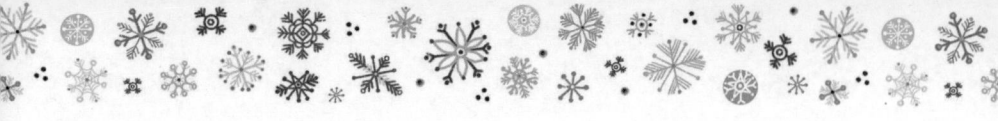

Soraya lingered behind as the rest of her class, including Christoff and Naomi, rushed off. She wanted a moment to appreciate the landscape, which looked like some faraway planet. The mountains ringed around them as if they were watching and protecting the lodge.

She got another idea for the new comic book she was working on about the snow-planet—maybe it could be full of ice-worm monsters that made tunnels underground.

"Come on, Soraya," Christoff called. The snowball fight was getting more energetic by the second.

"In a minute," she called back.

She couldn't wait to get back to her sketchpad and draw some ice worms. Maybe if her mom was busy with the play after dinner, she would get to draw by the fire.

She glanced at her class. The snowball fight had split into two teams. They'd somehow already built a snowy wall to separate one team from the other.

"How come you kids are never this organized in class?" she heard Mr. Haroyan shout.

As kids launched snowball after snowball over the wall, Soraya inched away from the others. She headed toward the steep, icy hill facing the lodge grounds. Between the high snowbanks, she'd noticed a narrow little passage leading into the hillside. There was something cozy and magical about it.

She slipped inside. She was careful not to go too far. She wanted her class to be able to hear her if there was an avalanche and she needed to yell for help.

She'd been right. It was cozy in the snow alley—like her own quiet little world.

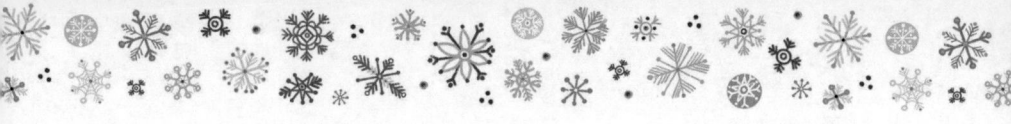

Suddenly, a sound echoed from further down the passage, where it turned a corner. Soraya jumped in surprise and forgot all about how cozy the snow alley had seemed.

An invisible voice spoke.

The Face in the Mountain

"Are you running away, too?" the voice said.

Soraya almost screamed, but stuffed her mittened hands in her mouth instead—she had heard that avalanches could be caused by screams.

She started to back out of the crevice when a face poked around the corner.

"Hello," said the face. "Why are they throwing snow at each other out there?"

Soraya staggered back and plastered herself to the side of the snowy passage. The thing stepped out from behind the corner and stood at the end of the passage, facing her in full view. It looked like a cross between a bear and a flat-nosed dog, but a very odd bear—one that had shaggy, all-white fur, stood upright, was about six feet tall, and could talk. Its big, blinking blue eyes were surrounded by dark lashes.

The longer she looked, the more she realized the creature didn't really look like a bear, either. The hairs on the back of her neck rose up.

A phrase came to mind, one that didn't really make her feel better.

"Abominable snowman," she murmured, without realizing she'd said it out loud. Her legs shook.

"See!" the creature said. He leapt back, quivering. "See, *this* is why."

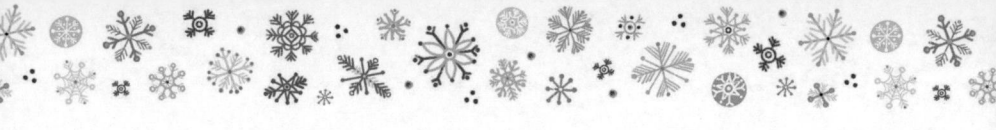

"Why *what*?" Soraya glanced behind her at her class. She realized they were yelling too loud to hear the creature, and she hoped he wouldn't try to eat her.

The creature put his paws (which ended in enormous, sharp-looking claws) to his mouth and glanced fearfully past Soraya at the rigorous snowball fight.

"'Abominable snowman' is an unfair label," he said, whimpering. "I reject labels."

Soraya and the creature stared at each other, and she saw that his eyes were huge with anxiety. Some of her own terror melted away. She had enough experience with otherworldly beings to know that this one probably wasn't going to lunge at her and kill her.

Probably.

"Well, *are* you an abominable snowman?" she said bluntly.

"*No.*" The creature stomped his shaggy foot. "That's a very offensive term. The correct term is *yeti*. Do I *look* abominable to you?"

The yeti bit his lip. He was clearly afraid she was going to say he *did* look abominable.

She considered. If this was a yeti, he seemed like a young yeti. She didn't know exactly why she thought that, except that his eyes were so big and his features seemed a little softer than what she imagined when she thought of a full-grown yeti. He also looked—she wasn't sure if this was the right word since he was so shaggy—a little bit thin?

"Uh—no. You don't look abominable," she said. She didn't add that she was pretty sure that once he was fully grown, he would definitely look abominable.

The yeti relaxed. "Yes," he said. "I don't think I do, either." He peered past her at her class.

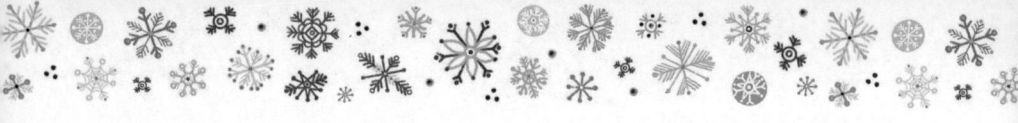

Soraya looked over her shoulder just in time to see Christoff launch himself like a torpedo at Derek.

"They look like they're really mad at each other," the creature said, his lip quivering. "Are they always like that? I thought humans were peaceful."

"Um," said Soraya. "Sometimes humans are peaceful. But not always."

"What about them?" The yeti pointed his claw at her class. "Are *they* usually peaceful?"

Soraya thought of Katie and Katie 2.0. "Well, they're not usually throwing snowballs, if that helps."

The yeti nodded intently. "I knew it. The human world is good. I thought that it would be. But I was hiding just in case the stuff my parents said is true."

"Your parents? So you *are* a kid yeti?" Soraya asked, hoping she wouldn't offend him.

He paused, then nodded, wide-eyed.

"What are you doing here?"

He stuck out his lip. "I ran away."

Before Soraya could respond to that, something rumbled. She jumped, thinking it was either the beginning of an avalanche or the yeti growling at her.

Instead, the yeti rubbed his stomach. "Sorry," he said.

"Are you—are you *hungry*?" Soraya said. She backed up a step.

"I don't want to eat *you*," the yeti said, looking hurt again. "Why do humans assume they would make a delicious meal?"

"Okay, I'm sorry. Why did you run away?" Soraya asked, peering into the passage again. "Where are your parents?"

The yeti gave a fearful yelp and scrambled backwards.

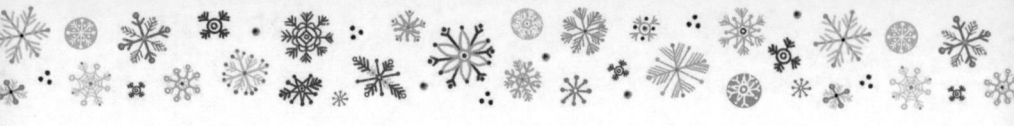

"Don't tell my parents I'm here—don't you tell them you saw me!" he cried, and then he dived back behind the corner in the passage.

"Okay, okay. Just be *quiet*," Soraya said, following him to the end of the crevice. "I can try to get you some foo—"

She peeked around the corner where the passage led further into the mountain.

The yeti was nowhere to be seen.

Soraya turned and bolted out of the passage, moving as fast as she could in her bubble-parka. She ignored the snowballs whistling past her head as she tottered across the snowy field in front of the lodge, right up to Naomi and Christoff.

Naomi was panting from the snow battle. "Where have you been?" she asked, just as a snowball splattered her cheek. She whirled around. "I know that was you, Katie. I'll get you for that!"

Before Naomi could assemble a snowball of her own, Soraya grabbed her friend's hand.

"Come with me," Soraya said under her breath. "Right now. You too, Christoff. I need your help—you'll never believe what I just saw."

Discovery

Christoff and Naomi's eyes grew bigger and bigger as Soraya told the story. Someone hurled a snowball at Christoff's back and he didn't even notice.

"A *yeti*," Naomi said, glancing toward the passage. "That's incredible!"

"What are the chances we'd meet *another* creature?" Christoff's eyes shone. "I gotta say, Soraya, before I started hanging out with you, the most exciting thing I met was a hedgehog in a pet store."

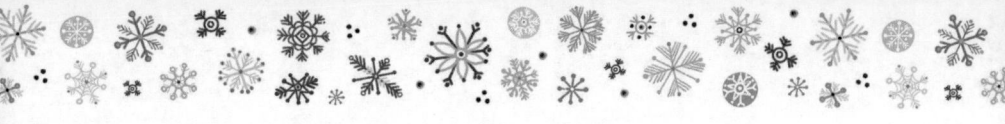

Soraya stared at her friends. How had she ended up with two friends who just *believed* her? They didn't ask her if she was sure about what she'd seen. They just believed her.

She could imagine what her mom would say if Soraya tried to tell her she'd just seen a yeti. Her mom would get mad at her for lying.

Her mom definitely hadn't believed that Soraya had met a mermaid during her class's field trip to the aquarium last fall. The mermaid, Estelle, had been accidentally trapped in one of the tanks. Soraya helped Estelle escape back to the sea and they became great friends.

Estelle was at home in the ocean now. Soraya missed her all the time, but she had learned better than to talk to her mom about her mythical friends. When Soraya, Naomi, and Christoff befriended Humphrey the dragon on their field trip to Balabrook Caverns, Soraya never mentioned it to her mom.

And her dad...Soraya's thoughts grew dark. She wasn't sure what her dad would say, since she hadn't seen him in years. He'd left her and her mom a long time ago.

In Soraya's opinion, the most likely explanation was that *she* was the reason her dad had left. Whenever she thought about it, her chest hurt. If she ever told *him* she saw a yeti...he'd probably leave the country just to get away from her.

"Soraya?" said Naomi. "Hello? We were talking about the yeti?"

"Oh, right." Soraya cleared her throat and hoped it wasn't too obvious that she had been completely lost in her thoughts. "I think the yeti's just a kid. A *big* kid. We have to help him."

"Of course we do," agreed Naomi, glancing back at the passage. "It sounds like he was quite distraught."

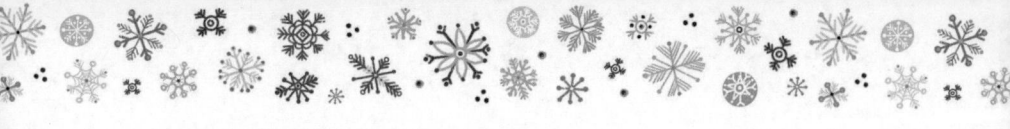

Distraught. Soraya liked that word. She made a mental note to herself to put it in her comic book.

"He was," she agreed. "He looked like he was too young to be out on his own. He also said he heard humans are peaceful."

Christoff's eyebrows shot up. "Then he definitely needs our help before he ends up trusting too many humans."

"He was *really* hungry," said Soraya.

"What do yetis eat?" said Christoff. "Or do I even want to know?"

"Do you think he'd eat *us* if he got hungry enough?" said Naomi.

Soraya paused. "No, I don't think so. He said he doesn't want to eat humans. Plus, if he wanted to eat me, he could have."

"That's reassuring," said Christoff. "Maybe yetis don't start eating people until they get older and bigger."

"Or maybe they don't eat people at all," Naomi pointed out. "We don't really know anything about yetis."

"That's true," said Christoff. "They might eat icicles for all we know."

"Well, we can't look for him right now." Naomi eyed the teachers and chaperones trying to wrangle everyone to go back inside. "Dinner's in a few minutes."

"Let's go back outside late tonight when everyone's in bed," Soraya said. "We can sneak some food to him."

Christoff and Naomi nodded as the three of them trooped back toward the snowball fight.

Soraya kept glancing over at the snowy passage, wondering if the yeti was watching.

* * *

Soraya wished she could have appreciated the delicious dinner laid out in the big dining hall that night, but all she could think about was the yeti. She, Christoff, and Naomi had all brought their own lunch bags with them, which they stuffed full of food under the table when no one was

looking. Soraya ended up with a bag crammed with corn, bread, turkey, baked potatoes, and green beans.

"Isn't this lovely, Soraya?" Soraya's mom said, looking around.

"Yeah, it's pretty," Soraya had to admit.

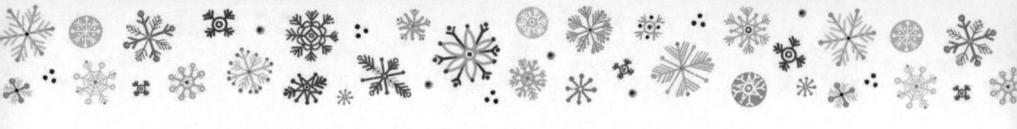

A fire flickered in a huge fireplace along one wall of the enormous dining room. Along the opposite wall, the stage stood behind thick, red velvet curtains. Other hotel guests were enjoying after-dinner hot chocolate.

Toward the end of the meal, everyone looked pleasantly drowsy—everyone except for Soraya, Naomi, and Christoff. They sat, alert, on the edges of their seats.

Ms. Staples stood up and raised a glass of sparkling water. "May I have everyone's attention? First of all, thank you to the Alpine Lodge for making us feel so welcome. We've had a lovely afternoon."

Everyone clapped.

"Tomorrow morning," Ms. Staples went on, "we'll go skiing on the mountain. I encourage you all to try it—there's nothing quite like it, and after all, that's why we're here. After lunch, there will be a rehearsal for our play,

The Snow Queen. As you know, the lodge is letting us use their beautiful stage. We'll be doing a dress rehearsal tomorrow evening during dinner. If you're not already a part of the production and you want to participate, please see Soraya's mom, Ms. Kadar, who's organizing and directing the play for us."

"Yes, please come see me if you'd like to help out." To Soraya's deep embarrassment, her mom leapt to her feet. "We can always use extra people to work on costumes, props, and set decoration."

Several kids got up and swarmed Soraya's mom, asking to be in the play. Apparently, something about the stage was so magical that it had inspired them.

Soraya nudged Christoff and Naomi. The sun had set outside the dining hall windows. Soraya trembled with anticipation.

"I got so much food for the yeti," Christoff said. "I hope he likes pecan pie."

"Soraya," her mom said, "are you sure you three don't want to help with the play? It would be so much fun."

"Sorry, Mom." Soraya shifted in her seat and looked at the floor. "I told you, I really hate being on stage."

"Me too," said Naomi. "I don't like being the center of attention."

"Me neither," Christoff said with a cough. Soraya and Naomi glanced sideways at him, their eyebrows raised.

"All right." Soraya could tell her mom was disappointed. "Just remember there's a spot for you if you change your mind."

"We will, Mom, thanks," said Soraya. "I'm sure you'll do a great job."

She stuffed another potato into her bag, hoping the yeti wasn't starving out there.

Basil

That night, while people were distracted with board games, Naomi managed to lug the three friends' coats and boots down the stairs without anyone seeing. She stashed them in the kitchen, which led to the grounds behind the lodge.

Soraya had volunteered to go with Naomi, but Naomi insisted that one person would look less suspicious than two.

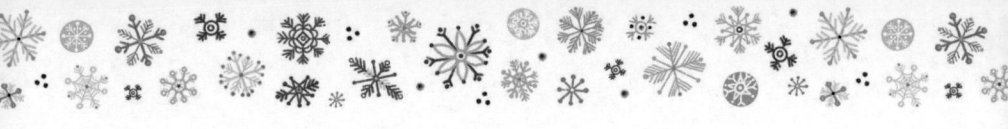

"All done," Naomi said when she returned, breathless. She sat down with Christoff and Soraya, who were hunched in the lobby by the fire, pretending to play chess. "There's no way we could have sneaked down the stairs wearing those things. They make too much noise."

"That was a brilliant idea, Naomi," said Christoff.

"Yeah, good thinking," said Soraya. She moved her pencil across her sketchbook page, keeping a sharp eye on the dining hall doorway in case her mom came out.

Christoff peered at her sketch. "That's so cool, Soraya."

"Thanks," Soraya said, beaming. She'd only recently started sharing her comics with her friends. "It's a comic about an ice planet with ice worms underground."

Soon they all headed upstairs. It seemed to take forever for everyone to go to bed.

Soraya's mom checked on them twice before she finally went off to her room.

When the lodge was quiet at last, Soraya and Naomi rose silently and slipped out into the hall in their socks, holding the bags of food they'd managed to steal from dinner. Christoff walked out of his bedroom door at the same time. As he opened it, Derek's droning snores came wafting out.

"I'm spending the rest of the night in the hall," Christoff whispered.

"C'mon," said Soraya, grateful for the little hall lamps that lit their way as they tiptoed down the long corridor.

They managed to sneak down two flights of stairs, staying out of sight of the front desk. Then they turned and went through the door to the basement kitchen.

"It's so...big and cold and empty," Soraya remarked, eyeing the sleek stainless steel countertops. Appliances whirred softly.

"Here." Naomi fished their coats out of a large supply closet. "Put them on, quick."

"What if the yeti's not out there?" said Christoff, pulling on his orange penguin coat.

"Then we'll just leave him the food." Soraya wrestled herself into her bubbly parka. "I'm sure he's the only hungry yeti out there."

"Oh, this is good *and* bad," said Naomi, once they stepped out of the back door and onto the snowy lawn. "The moon is bright enough that we won't need extra light, but it also means people will be able to see us if they look out the windows."

Soraya glanced back at the lodge. Her mom would probably have a heart attack if she caught Soraya sneaking across the grounds in the middle of the night.

"Let's hurry." Naomi plunged into the snowy field.

The night was freezing, but at least it wasn't snowing. The three of them hurried as quickly as they could across the moonlit grounds toward the crevice in the mountain where Soraya had seen the yeti.

"Remember," Soraya whispered, "don't ask the yeti about his parents, or you might make him run away again."

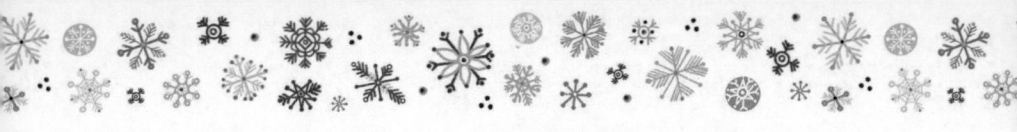

When they'd ducked safely into the passage, out of sight of the lodge, she held up a bag of food. "Little yeti…hey, little yeti, come out! It's us, um, peaceful humans. We brought you something to eat."

At first, there was silence. Then, the yeti suddenly poked his head out from the end of the passage.

Naomi gasped.

Christoff said, "*Dude.*"

The yeti stepped all the way into the passage, as he had done earlier that day. Soraya could have sworn he had grown an inch or two since that morning. Now his stomach growled constantly.

"He doesn't look so little to me," Naomi whispered.

"I'm glad you're still here," Soraya said. "Here's some food that we brought for you."

She lay her food bag on the ground near the yeti. "Bread…four apples…turkey…potatoes…"

"Pecan pie and green beans," Christoff added, placing his own bag next to Soraya's. "Sorry about the beans. I had to go for whatever I could reach at the table without anyone seeing me."

"I have some corn on the cob," Naomi said. "And cheesecake."

The yeti stared at the food they'd laid out, his eyes wide. Then his gaze landed on the turkey and his ears drooped.

"You all thought I'd like to devour meat," he said sadly. "Because I'm a terrible, scary monster."

The yeti wiped his eyes with the back of one huge paw.

"No, no—we weren't sure," Soraya said quickly. "We brought a little of everything."

"I don't eat meat," the yeti said weakly. "I...I've turned a corner." He lifted his trembling chin. "I don't wish to be a monstrous carnivore, no matter what anyone thinks."

Quickly, Soraya put the meat behind her. "There are crackers in there."

"And a chocolate bar," said Naomi.

"And the pie," offered Christoff.

The young yeti stared at them hungrily. He scooted forward, grabbed the food, and scrambled back again. "I'm a vegetarian," he announced, stuffing a whole apple into its mouth.

"Don't forget to spit out the core," Christoff suggested.

"Um...are yetis usually vegetarian like you?" Naomi asked.

"I'm an outlier," the yeti said, his mouth full of corn, pie, and beans, all at the same time.

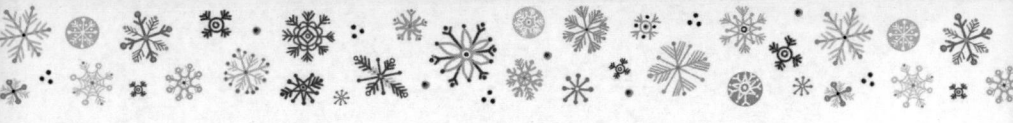

"Do you like that word, *outlier*? I discovered it this morning. I found some books someone had thrown into the dumpster at the lodge." He shook its head in disbelief. "Can you imagine throwing away a book?"

"Wait..." Soraya's heart thumped. "You went to the dumpster? That's really close to the lodge. Someone could have seen you!"

"They wouldn't believe a yeti can read?" said the yeti.

"Well, they'd probably be more concerned about the fact that you exist in the first place," Christoff said.

"Why?" said the yeti, biting into some cheesecake. "I'm very nice."

Soraya felt herself wanting to hug the yeti, but she held back.

"What's your name?" she asked instead.

"Basil," said the yeti. "It's a noble name for a boy yeti."

"Where are your par—" Naomi started to say, but then she remembered what Soraya had said and caught herself. "Where did you come from?"

Basil shrugged. "The top of Mount Bergen, of course," he said.

"And why did you leave?" said Christoff.

Basil hung his head and chewed his cheesecake sadly. "You'd leave, too, if your parents wanted you to be monstrous. I don't want to be monstrous. 'It's your destiny,' they always say. 'Your job is to scare people, just as we've always done.'" Basil's eyes flashed. "But what if I don't feel it's my destiny? What if I don't *want* to be abominable?"

He angrily bit into the cheesecake. Tears wobbled in his eyes.

"So, the other yetis want you to be scary, but you don't want to be?" asked Christoff. "That's why you ran away?"

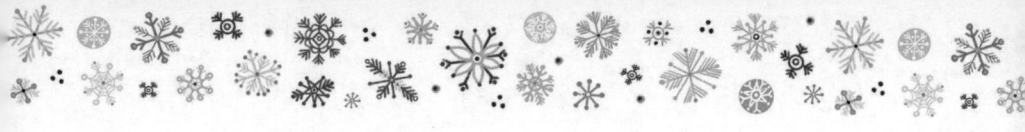

"Yes," said Basil, sniffling. "I'm a pacifist. I want to write poetry."

"I love poetry!" said Soraya. "What kind do you want to write?"

"All kinds." Basil perked up and his eyes shone. "Poems about the beauty of the stars. About sunsets and rain. About how peaceful humans are."

"We're not—" Christoff started to say, but Naomi shot him a look.

"Have you told your family that you want to be a poet?" said Naomi.

"They don't understand me," said Basil. "They think I'm giving up on my duty of being a good monster. They don't even like poetry."

"But if you're running away, what are you doing here in this passage?" Soraya asked.

"I'm waiting," said Basil. He licked some cheesecake off his claws and squared his shoulders. "I want to go to…Panama."

"*Panama?*" said Christoff.

Basil nodded. A giant smile lit up his face. "They have coconuts in Panama."

"How do you even know about Panama?" said Naomi.

"I read about it in a travel magazine I got out of the dumpster," said Basil. "When I'm in Panama, I'll eat coconuts and write all the poetry I want."

Soraya's head spun. She glanced at the others. They looked as crestfallen as she felt.

"Um, Basil," said Naomi. "How were you planning to get to Panama?"

"I'll go with a human, of course," he said. "They can take me! Mama Yeti and Papa Yeti said humans are *not* great and that I should hide from them. That's why I hid at first. But now I know humans *are* great! Soraya told me so."

"I never said humans are *great*," Soraya said. "And...how did you get all the way down the mountain without anyone seeing you? How can yetis hide when you're so big?"

"We're really good at camouflage. We can stand perfectly still and blend in when we want to," Basil said proudly, still stuffing his face with food. "Plus, we use magic."

"Um, Basil, we should tell you..." said Christoff. "Humans might disappoint you a little. I don't know if you'll find someone to take you to Panama."

"I'll do whatever I want!" Basil cried, scrambling to his feet. "I'm sick of everyone telling me what to do. I'll find a way to get to Panama, just wait and see."

Soraya's heart raced with panic. "Basil," she said, "promise me you won't walk up to any humans and ask them to take you to Panama."

"In fact, don't walk up to any humans, period," said Naomi, wrinkling her brow

in concern. "I'm afraid most humans won't understand you. They'll be scared of you."

"But *you're* not scared of me." Basil blinked as he looked at each of them.

"Well, yeah...but we're a little different," said Christoff.

"They don't need to be scared." Basil gazed longingly past them toward the lodge. His lip quivered. "I write *poetry*. I'm a *vegetarian*."

Soraya's palms were sweating now. "Listen, Basil," she said, "we'll figure out a way to help you, okay? And we'll bring you food in the meantime. Just promise that you'll wait for us, and that you won't try to go near any other humans."

"You'll take me to Panama?" he said. "Where I can get a coconut?"

Naomi hesitated. "We'll do everything we can. We promise that."

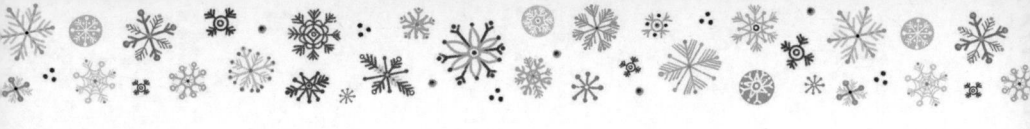

"The hotel kitchen might even have a coconut we could bring you," Christoff said. "But you'll have to wait here for it."

Basil sat down again warily and picked up the pecan pie.

Soraya glanced back at the lodge. "We have to go now, but we'll bring you more food tomorrow, okay?"

Basil nodded, tucking into the pie. Soon it was smeared all over his grizzly white face.

"Just stay put," said Christoff.

The three kids hurried out of the passage, leaving Basil sitting in the middle of his half-devoured feast.

"Poor little yeti," Soraya said, wringing her hands as they plodded back across the snow. "Or, poor big little yeti."

"If he keeps coming near the lodge and someone sees him, they'll take him away to experiment on him," Naomi said quietly.

"It's the same thing your friend Estelle was afraid of."

Soraya had told Christoff and Naomi all about her mermaid friend. Estelle had been positive that if she were discovered, people would keep her prisoner so they could study her and do experiments on her. Soraya couldn't imagine a worse fate.

"They would *definitely* experiment on him," Christoff said. "And put him on display. Plus, this whole place would get torn apart with everyone looking for more yetis."

Soraya balled up her fists inside her mittens. "We're going to help Basil no matter what. Or," she said quickly, "*I* will. You don't have to help."

"Not this again," said Naomi, rolling her eyes. During their trip to the cavern, Soraya had been reluctant to accept help from Christoff and Naomi on her mission to reunite Humphrey the dragon with his family.

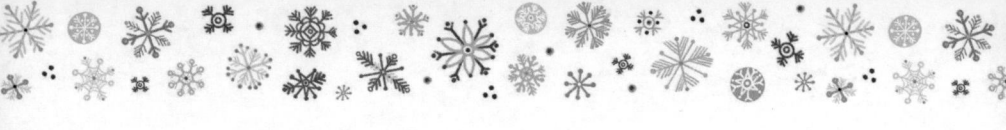

"We're in this together, Soraya," said Christoff. "Why else would I sneak out with you two in the middle of the night? We're *all* going to help Basil."

They sneaked back into the lodge and peeled off their coats and boots. As they crept past the lobby, they saw a guard standing near the front doors. He was holding up a pointed object with liquid inside—it looked like he was checking the amount of liquid.

"Hey, what's that for?" Soraya blurted out, unable to stop herself.

The guard turned. He looked a little wild-eyed—so jumpy and distracted that he didn't seem to notice that the three friends were lugging around their outdoor clothes, which were covered in melting snow.

"A few bear sightings were reported near the lodge. We're on the lookout now, so don't worry, kids," he said. "One tranquilizer dart like this one is enough to make even a full-grown bear fall asleep if it comes close again!"

Mount Bergen

"I hope you all are excited to go skiing," Soraya's mom said as she hurried down to breakfast the next morning. The students were buzzing excitedly about getting to go out on the slopes.

Soraya, Christoff, and Naomi nibbled at their pancakes and eggs. None of them felt like eating. They were too scared for Basil—especially now that guards were on the lookout for "bears." They were sure someone had seen Basil and thought he was a bear.

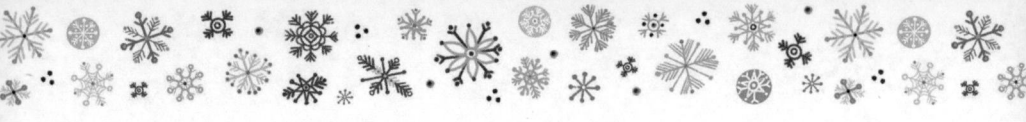

But Naomi had convinced them that they needed to eat so they could keep up their strength to help Basil. While they were eating, they were also trying to stuff bits of pancake into plastic bags Naomi had snagged from the kitchen.

"Actually, Ms. Kadar," Naomi said, "I think I might skip out on the skiing. I'm not feeling so well." She made a convincing cough.

Soraya nodded as she gulped down orange juice. "Me too," she said. "I'll stay here and play solitaire."

"Yeah, I just remembered," Christoff said with his mouth full of pancakes, "my ankle's been really sore. Soccer accident."

Soraya's mom raised an eyebrow. "Your ankle seemed fine yesterday during the snowball fight, when you took out about ten of your classmates," she pointed out.

Christoff smiled weakly and shrugged.

Soraya's mom sighed. "Listen, Soraya, you don't have to love skiing. But the PTA worked all year to raise the money for this trip. I want you to try it at least once. If you hate it, you don't have to do it again, but get out there at least once. It's fun."

"*Mom...*" Soraya said.

"No whining about it, Soraya. If you hate skiing after today, you never have to go again. But I'd like you to try it this morning." She checked her watch. "Your classes are meeting Mr. Haroyan and some of the chaperones in the lobby in fifteen minutes, so you kids need to go put on your ski clothes now."

Soraya, Naomi, and Christoff exchanged looks of despair. They hurried out of the lobby and up the stairs, their clothes bulging with hidden bags of food.

"We won't have time to bring Basil anything to eat before we go," Soraya said.

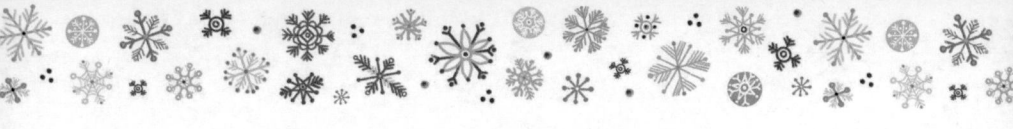

"Yeah, and this was a good haul." Christoff opened his jacket to show them three enormous bags of pancakes. "It would be a shame for it to go to waste."

"There's an ice machine in the hall by the vending machine," said Naomi. "We could stash the food in there to keep it fresh and hope no one finds it until we get back."

They stuffed the food into the hallway ice machine. Ten minutes later, they walked down the stairs into the lobby wearing their parkas, snow pants, ski goggles, and helmets. They went to the equipment rental place in the hotel lobby, picked up their ski boots and skis, and pulled on the boots. Then their class—along with three parents, Mr. Haroyan, and some ski instructors—trooped off toward the ski lift.

"We're so *close*," Christoff whispered to Soraya and Naomi. "I wish we could've just brought the food and sneaked it out to Basil real quick!"

Soraya gazed longingly at the snowy crevice where she assumed Basil was still hiding, waiting for them.

"And *I* wish yetis were telepathic," Soraya whispered back as they clambered onto a gondola on the ski lift. It was just wide enough to fit the three of them. "Then I could tell him we'll be there soon."

Naomi suddenly sucked in her breath. "Oh my gosh, *look*."

She pointed directly across from the lodge, to the crevice in the snow. A shaggy white face was sticking out and peering around.

"Oh no." Soraya leaned out as far as she could safely go. "*Basil, get back.*"

It was useless, of course. Basil couldn't hear her. She gestured frantically.

Naomi tugged her sleeve, pointing at the other people climbing into the gondola behind them.

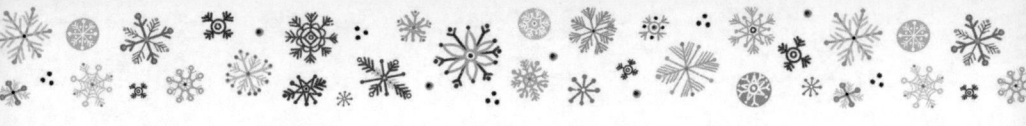

As the gondola lifted them up toward the top of the mountain, Soraya had no choice but to sit back and try not to glance at the crevice, even though her stomach churned with anxiety.

The ski lift lurched on. Everyone chatted and laughed, except Soraya, Christoff, and Naomi. They exchanged anguished glances as the lift took them farther and farther up the mountain.

Soraya couldn't even enjoy the majestic landscape spreading out below them. She gazed down at tall, snow-covered pines as they went up, up into what felt like the clouds.

When everyone slid off the gondolas, some ski instructors were waiting for them.

"Welcome!" one of the instructors called out. "Now, let's get started with our first lesson. This way to the green trail. It's the easiest trail on the mountain so it's a good one for you to practice on, once we give you a few pointers."

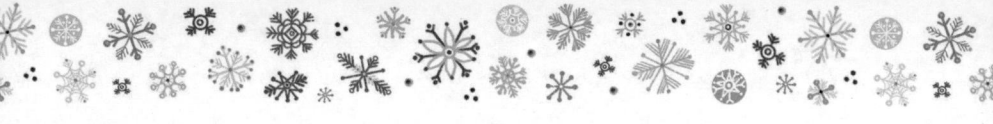

Soraya huddled with Christoff and Naomi, feeling awkward in her skis. No one was nearby, so she was able to talk to her friends freely. "I hope Basil stays put so no one sees him."

"Me, too," muttered Christoff. "Let's get this over with as quickly as possible." He nodded down at his skis.

"Wait a minute," said Naomi. "Didn't Basil say his family lives up here? If that's true, and people are up here all the time, how come no one's reported seeing any yetis?"

"He said yetis have ways they can make sure they're not found, if they don't want to be," Soraya said confidently. "Remember? He said they use camouflage and magic."

"Okay," said the instructor. "The first thing we'll learn is how to position our skis. We'll learn a position called 'pizza' and another one called 'French fries.' 'Pizza' is pointing the front of your skis together into a wedge shape, like this, so your skis make a triangle,

like a slice of pizza. 'French fries' is when you position your skis parallel to each other, like this."

Soraya didn't feel as comfortable on her skis as Naomi and Christoff seemed to feel on theirs. When the instructor finally told them it was all right to go, she took off and slid clumsily down the gently sloping green trail.

She had to admit there *was* something fun about gliding on top of the snow. She was behind almost everyone else in the class, except for Christoff and Naomi, who skied on either side of her.

Another trail forked off of the green trail. Suddenly Soraya couldn't remember if she was supposed to 'French fry' or 'pizza' in order to stay straight, and she found herself skidding onto the other trail. She wobbled on her skis, whizzed down the steeper slope—and the next thing she knew, she careened into the pine forest on one side of the path.

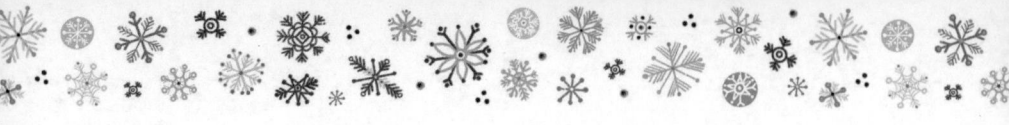

"Soraya!" she heard Naomi call out from behind her.

Soraya didn't know how to stop or turn around. She kept gliding along, terrified, narrowly avoiding tree trunks. Flakes of snow flew all around her, which was strange since it hadn't been snowing before. Finally, her ski got caught on a root and she toppled over.

Somewhere close by, she heard Christoff shout, "Ow!"

"Are you all right? Christoff, Soraya, where are you?" Naomi's voice sounded panicked. "Where *are* we?"

That was a good question. Soraya sat up and wiped snow out of her eyes. This didn't look like any part of the trail that she'd seen. It was dense with whirling snow. Ahead of them, she could see a path. Hairs rose on the back of her neck. She sensed something odd that she couldn't quite explain.

"Soraya, where are you?" Naomi called again. Her footsteps crunched in the snow.

"Over here." Soraya reached down and popped her ski boots out of her skis. Christoff and Naomi struggled through the snowy trees toward her. Both of them had also removed their skis.

"Hold still," said Soraya. "Do you feel that?"

Christoff hugged himself like he had sudden chills.

"Yeah," he whispered, his eyes wide. "What do you think it is?"

Soraya pushed herself up onto her feet. "It's magic. It's *got* to be. There's magic somewhere close."

"This snow doesn't make any sense," said Naomi, protecting her eyes from the cold, blowing flakes. "It wasn't snowing at all back on the trail. Why would there be a totally different weather system in these woods?"

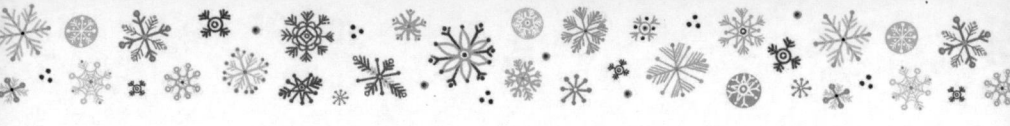

Soraya squeaked. "Look!" she said. The dense snow whirled into the shape of a tunnel. Far down the tunnel, a towering, shaggy white creature lumbered along the path away from them. The ground vibrated each time its foot hit the ground.

She gripped her friends' hands without a word until the creature had disappeared at the end of the weird, swirling snow-tunnel.

"Did you see that?" Christoff whispered at last. "Because I saw that. It looked like—like a stretched-out version of Basil."

"It's one of the other yetis," Naomi said softly. "A grown-up one."

Soraya's heart pounded. "*This* must be how they keep any humans from seeing them. I think it—it must be sort of like a magic entrance that leads to wherever they are." She took a deep breath. "Let's go after it."

"*Basil* might be nice, but that thing didn't look like it would hesitate to eat us," Christoff protested.

"Christoff's right, Soraya," Naomi said nervously. "There's no guarantee that the other yetis are as nice as Basil."

"I just have a weird sense that we should follow," said Soraya. "Also, if they're Basil's relatives, maybe we can figure out why he left. We can stay out of sight."

She headed into the whirling snow at the edge of the tunnel.

"How are we going to stay out of sight? We're wearing snow gear that's every color of the rainbow!" Christoff said.

He had a point.

Soraya crossed her arms. "We'll just have to do our best," she said.

Christoff sighed. "Okay, Soraya, but we are *staying quiet*."

They crept further into the tunnel, trying as hard as possible not to make a sound in their clunky ski boots.

From up ahead, Soraya could hear wailing, thunderous sounds. The sounds started to take shape until she realized they were voices—big, booming voices and high, screeching voices.

Christoff froze behind her. *We should go back*, he mouthed silently.

Soraya shook her head and tugged them onward. Up ahead was the sharp edge of a tall hill or cliff. If they could hide behind it and peek around the corner without being seen, they might be able to observe whatever was making the noises.

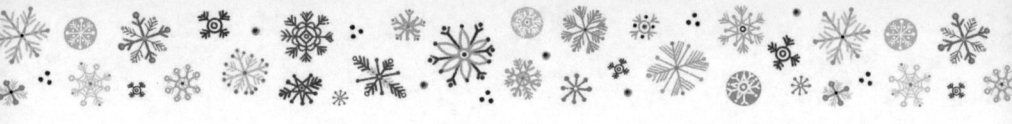

Finally, they were at the cliffside. Soraya inched along, feeling her way along the rock and trying to stay flat against it. The others inched behind her.

She took a deep breath and peeked around the side. She was tempted to scream, but managed to restrain herself.

She peered at several huge creatures gathered in a circle in a snowy clearing. They were at least twelve feet tall and covered in thick, shaggy, white fur. Some of them sat on piles of snow or rocks, and others paced around restlessly. The ground shook a little every time one of them took a step.

Soraya glanced back at Naomi and Christoff, who were both paralyzed with fear.

"You didn't find anything, then?" said one of the yetis glumly.

"No! I searched the whole mountain again, from top to bottom," said another yeti,

flinging herself down onto a rock. "This is my fault. The life we provided him wasn't good enough."

"What are you talking about? You're a great mom, and he had everything a yeti could want," cried a shorter, more grizzled yeti. "A loving family! Our rich culture! Our wonderful traditions! A great location for scaring humans!"

"It's true," said still another yeti. "We could have chosen any mountain for our home. But we settled here, where we could be close to humans. Wonderful, lily-livered humans. And he doesn't appreciate any of it!"

The mother yeti wiped her eyes and looked up from the rock she was sitting on. "We're still assuming he left on purpose. He *could* have gotten lost. My boy never had the best sense of direction."

"I doubt it," said the grizzled yeti. "Young 'uns are mischievous."

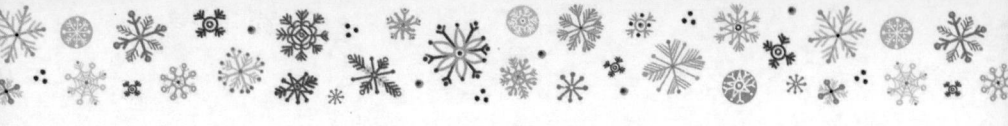

"If Basil did run away, he'll come back. I know he will," said the mother yeti. "My son's a good boy. I bet once he realizes what he's missing, he'll come home. He probably can't go three days without a nice chance to scare humans."

"Regardless," said the older yeti, "if he's not back soon, we'll have to expand our search beyond the mountain."

If Soraya hadn't already been holding her breath, she would have gasped. Christoff and Naomi looked at each other in alarm.

"Let's get out of here, now!" Christoff whispered.

As quietly as they could, they crept back along the steep cliff, and once again into the strange tunnel of snow. Soraya was terrified that any second she would hear booming yeti footsteps behind her, but they made it safely to the end of the tunnel. Tripping in their ski

boots, they walked right back into the wooded spot where they'd gone off the trail.

"I can't believe it." Gasping, Christoff fell back to sit on the cold ground. "I just can't... we almost became yeti lunch!"

"Well, they never said anything about *eating* humans." Naomi stumbled through the snow, searching among the trees. "We need to find our skis and hurry back. And make sure Basil's all right."

"They said they're going to expand their search." Christoff stood up. "Where did I leave my skis?"

"Over here with mine," Naomi called.

Soraya just sat. "They were so sad," she said softly. "His family."

She couldn't stop thinking about the worry and care in the yetis' voices. They definitely loved and missed Basil, even if they didn't quite understand him.

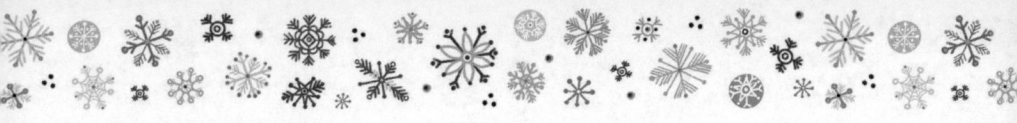

For some reason, Soraya thought of her sketchpad and her comic books hidden deep in her backpack at the lodge. She pushed the thought away.

"Come on, let's go," said Naomi.

The three of them scrambled out of the woods and back onto the trail. Soraya expected Mr. Haroyan or another adult to pop out and demand to know where they'd been, but no one did.

Instead, a few classmates glided by, their faces gleeful.

"This is awesome!" shouted Derek as he whizzed past them.

Christoff shook his head. "I can't believe we just *saw a yeti family* and no one has a clue."

Naomi peered down the mountain. "Come on. We'll finish skiing and then figure out what to do when we get back to the lodge."

Soraya didn't know how she got through the rest of the morning. All she could think about was the strange magical snow-tunnel, the family of yetis, and most of all, how anguished they had been about losing Basil.

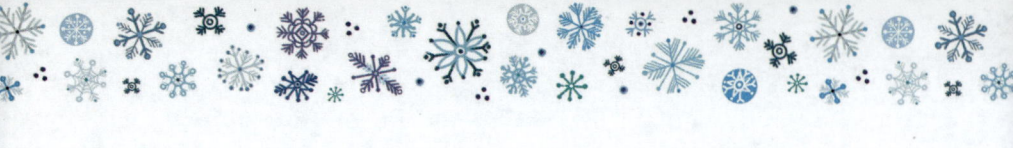

The Hunt

The minute the lodge came into view on their way back from skiing, Soraya could tell something was wrong. Several trucks with logos on them were in the lodge's driveway, but they were too far away for her to read the lettering. A commotion was in progress outside the front doors. Ms. Staples and the manager of the lodge, Ms. Wilber, stood there along with some other people.

"What's going on?" asked Mr. Haroyan as their class approached the entrance.

"We've had a *slight* issue this morning, nothing to worry about," said Ms. Wilber, her eyes darting nervously to each teacher and chaperone gathered outside the hotel.

Ms. Staples shot her a look. "It's a bit more than a slight issue." She turned to the class. "Now, listen. I don't want anyone to panic. But this morning, a student saw something inside the lodge that she thought looked like a wild animal. It was white and furry, so it could have been a white bear or a white wolf. Animal Control is here right now to search the lodge."

Soraya gasped. She heard Naomi and Christoff do the same.

"It's highly unlikely that a wild animal would find its way into the lodge," Ms. Wilber said in a high, wavering voice.

Katie stepped back. "So, some big bear could, like, *eat* us or something? Isn't that, like, illegal?"

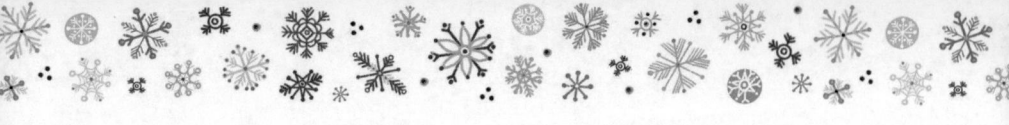

"Since when do bears care about laws, Katie?" said Elias.

Mara, one of the kids who hadn't gone skiing, burst out of the lodge. "Abby's the one who saw it! She said there was a big, shaggy, white bear inside the lodge!"

"Ew," said Katie 2.0. "That's super creepy. A bear *inside*."

"I think it's cool!" said Ling, who sounded way too excited.

"No white bears or wolves have ever been spotted inside this hotel, so this is definitely strange," said Ms. Wilber. "You can take my word for it that this is not a regular day at Alpine Lodge."

"It *wasn't* a bear—at least I don't think it was." Abby shuffled out the front doors. Her eyes were bright red and looked haunted. "It was standing up on its hind legs and it looked more like…a *monster*."

Soraya suddenly felt dizzy.

"Well, whatever it was, we take student concerns very seriously," said Ms. Staples. "So while Animal Control searches the lodge, we'll go straight into the dining hall to wait there. We've been assured we'll be safe if we stay there while they work."

The last part of what she said was drowned out; the whole class, including the parent chaperones, erupted in shouts and questions. All except for Christoff, Soraya, and Naomi, who stood stock-still, not daring to move.

"Shouldn't take too much longer." A man wearing an Animal Control uniform poked his head out of the front door. "Come on in, everyone. The path to the dining hall is all clear."

Mr. Haroyan sighed. "And I was hoping for a soothing trip. All right, quiet down, everyone! Let's cooperate so Animal Control can get this done as quickly as possible."

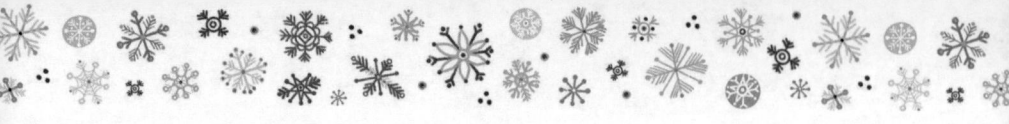

The parent chaperones hustled everyone inside, their faces anxious. As for the class, most of them craned their necks from side to side as they filed past the lobby to the dining hall, trying to catch a glimpse of whatever it was that Abby had seen.

"*Straight to the dining hall,*" Ms. Staples bellowed.

Soraya had to think fast. "Okay, can we all agree that we're not going to let Basil get captured by Animal Control?"

"Of course we won't," said Christoff, wiping sweat off his forehead. "But it looks as if the chaperones are about to lock us in the dining hall."

"Which is why we should try to escape now, while all this chaos is going on," said Naomi. She wrung her hands. "I hope Basil knows enough to hide from the Animal Control workers. What if he comes walking out and asks one of them to take him to Panama?"

Soraya's stomach dropped. "Let's hurry." She scoured the lobby. "We'll have to search the place before they do. If we make a run for it and hide near the elevator—"

"There you are!" Soraya's mom rushed up to them, her face pale with concern. "Thank goodness. I was worried sick about you three."

"Abby's got a big imagination, Mom," Soraya said as her mom crushed her in a hug. "Plus, her eyesight's not that great."

"Soraya, that little girl was shaken," her mom said. "You should have seen her."

"Parent chaperones, if we could have a word with you, please," Mr. Haroyan called out from the middle of the dining hall.

"Okay, gotta go." Soraya's mom gave her one more hug. "I'm just so glad you're safe."

They watched her elbow her way through the crowd.

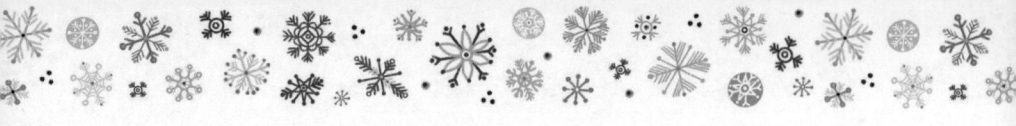

"*Now,*" said Soraya.

The three of them dashed for the doors, trying as best as they could to make it look as if they were just lost in the shuffle. But as soon as they were outside the dining hall and in the now-empty lobby, they bolted for the stairs.

They pounded up, pausing at the second-floor landing to look down the hallway. There were several Animal Control workers at the very end of the hall.

"Keep going!" Naomi said with a squeal.

They raced up the next flight of stairs to the third floor, where they hid behind a large upholstered chair near the staircase.

"Take off your coats—they make noise, and we need to be able to move," Naomi ordered. "Boots, too."

They peeled off their parkas and boots and stashed them under the chair.

"Feels great to be out of those things," said Christoff, wiggling his toes inside his socks.

"Okay, let's check every door," Soraya whispered, feeling almost sick with fear. "They'll search this floor next, and if he's up here, maybe we'll find him before they do!"

As fast as they possibly could, Christoff, Soraya, and Naomi knocked on door after door in the hallway, softly calling, "Basil! Basil, it's us. We just want to help you. We'll take you to Panama!"

They heard the Animal Control workers shouting from one floor below them. They didn't sound like people who'd react well to finding a yeti.

Soraya was panting when they met up at the end of the hall. "No luck."

"What's that?" Naomi pointed at an unmarked door they had missed. "Maybe it leads to the attic. Judging by how the lodge looks from outside, it's definitely got an attic."

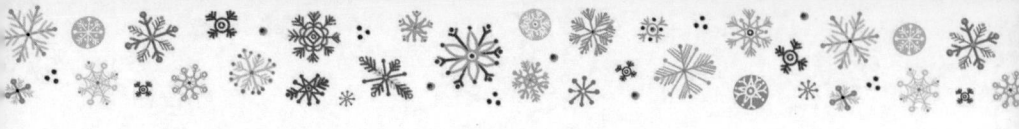

The three friends didn't waste any time. They dashed down the hall to the door and clomped up the narrow, musty staircase behind it. A door at the top of the stairs opened into a huge, lofty, and very dusty attic.

All kinds of stuff had been stashed up here—there were cleaning supplies, but also old furniture, globes, some telescopes, and old recliners that looked like they belonged to Sherlock Holmes. It was hotter in the attic than it was in the rest of the lodge. Right away, Soraya found herself sweating.

"This place is *cool*," Christoff said. "All right, hurry, let's start looking!"

Soraya felt there was little chance that Basil would have chosen to hide up here, but they stumbled frantically around the room, peeking into every corner.

"Oh my gosh," Naomi said. "Christoff, Soraya, come here!"

They rushed over to her.

Soraya's stomach flipped again: there, huddled in a corner behind an old foosball table, was Basil.

He was slumped against the wall, eyes half-closed, his fur droopy and matted.

"Basil!" Soraya dropped to her knees in front of him. "What's wrong? What happened?"

"I don't know," Basil said, barely able to whisper. "I came into the lodge because I was so hungry. I'm sorry. And I came up here after a girl saw me and started screaming. I—I remembered what you said about some people not being so nice. So I ran away from her and hid. But it's so hot…"

Soraya felt his shaggy forehead. "He's burning up!"

"Basil, I don't think you can survive out of the snow and ice," said Naomi. "The warmth is making you sick. We have to get you back outside where it's cold."

"No!" said Basil, with as much force as he could muster. "I won't go back home."

The three of them exchanged a glance. Soraya knew they were all thinking the same thing: they wouldn't mention the fact that they'd seen Basil's family until later.

"Okay, listen, Basil," said Soraya. "We'll talk about that after you are safe. Right now we just have to get you out of this heat."

"We can't put him outside in the snow in this condition for everyone to find. Who knows how long it'll take him to recover?" said Christoff. Then he snapped his fingers. "I know! The kitchen. It has a big freezer, right? We'll put him in there for a little while!"

"And then, after the freezer, you'll take me to Panama?" Basil said hopefully.

Soraya turned to the others helplessly. "But how are we supposed to smuggle him past Animal Control all the way to the *kitchen*? It's in the basement."

"Here." Naomi pulled a dusty old sheet off of a chair. "Sorry, Basil, it's going to be hot for a minute, but it'll cool down again right after that. We've got to cover you up in case anyone sees you on our way downstairs." She promptly started wrapping Basil in the sheet, signaling the others to help. When he was all wrapped up, Soraya said, "Okay, let's go."

They dragged poor Basil out of the attic, down the stairs, and into the third-floor hallway—where an Animal Control worker was just coming up the stairs, but fortunately looking down the other wing.

Thinking fast, Christoff pulled something out of his pocket and hurled it down the hall, toward the staircase. It bounced down the steps.

"My favorite yo-yo," he whispered.

"What was that?" The Animal Control guy spun around and raced down the steps after it. "Anyone else hear that sound?"

"Quick! The laundry chute," said Soraya.

The Animal Control worker might turn around and come back at any moment. The laundry chute was their only hope.

They raced down the hall to the chute with Basil stumbling along between them. Soraya had flashbacks of sneaking through the aquarium with her mermaid friend, Estelle, in a janitor's bucket.

They reached the chute just as they heard footsteps hammering back up the stairs.

In one single motion, all three of them hoisted Basil into the chute. It was, fortunately, a very large chute.

"Hey!" the Animal Control guy called, spotting them just as the chute swung shut. "You're all supposed to be in the dining hall."

"Sorry!" Christoff called back. "I—um—I puked on some sheets and I just wanted to put them in the laundry."

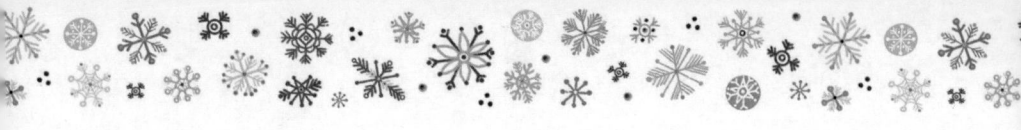

"That can wait." The Animal Control worker strode toward them. "You all are supposed to be down in—"

"We know, and we're going straight there now," said Christoff.

The three of them sidestepped the man and ran faster than they'd ever run. Christoff paused to snag his yo-yo from the staircase, and then they sprinted down three flights of stairs and slip-skidded into the basement.

"I think the laundry room is down this way," said Naomi, hurrying past the kitchen.

They burst into a large room with at least a dozen washers and dryers. And there, in the far wall, was the opening of the chute, right above a giant bin of dirty laundry. Laying on the very top of the pile was a huge sausage-shaped sheet with a tuft of white fur sticking out of the top.

"Basil!" Soraya unwrapped him as fast as she could and pulled him out of the bin.

He moaned. "It was weird in there."

Supporting Basil like human crutches, the three of them rushed him back down the hall to the kitchen. At any minute, adults might come looking for them—Soraya had no doubt that the Animal Control worker would go straight to the dining hall and tattle on them.

"There's the freezer," said Naomi. "Quick, Christoff, hold the door open for us."

They hauled Basil into the giant walk-in freezer. As soon as they were inside, Soraya and Naomi started shivering. But Basil's eyes cleared as they propped him against the frosty wall.

"Where am I?" he asked, blinking.

"The freezer in the kitchen," Soraya told him. "Basil, you'll have to stay here and hide until we can figure out how to help you. We'll be back in just a little bit."

Basil blinked. "You won't tell my parents where I am if you see them, will you?"

They looked at each other.

Soraya took a deep breath. "Basil, we have to hurry right now, but I just want to tell you something—we *did* see your family."

He shrank in fear. "You told on me!"

"No, we didn't tell. We were skiing and discovered your family by accident. They didn't see us. We heard them talking. And—they really miss you."

Basil jutted out his lip. He wiped tears from his eyes. "Maybe now you believe me about what they are like? They hate the magic of poetry!"

"Maybe you could teach them," said Christoff. "It can't hurt to try."

"You could try standing up for yourself to see if that works," Soraya added. She flushed at her own suggestion, but wasn't sure why. "You could tell them that you want to be a poet, and you don't want to scare people."

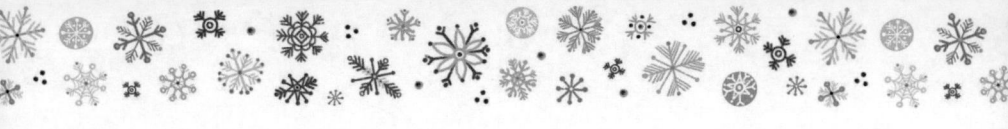

"You saw them," Basil said. "Imagine telling my fourteen-foot grandmother that you disagree with her."

Soraya looked down. "Well, yeah... I can see your point," she admitted.

Basil curled into a furry ball. "They'll hate me. Unless..." He brightened. "Will you come with me?"

Soraya squeaked. "What?"

"Will you all come with me when I talk to them? For moral support?" Basil beamed up at them. "You won't need to show yourselves. Just knowing that my three smart human friends are close by will give me courage. Since you all love poetry so much."

Soraya's heart twisted. The last thing she wanted to do was to possibly be discovered by a colony of towering, furious yetis. But she also couldn't very well show Basil that she was

scared of his family if she was telling him *not* to be afraid of them.

"Okay, we'll go with you," she said with a glance at the others, who looked green at the thought. "After Animal Control is gone, we'll take you back up to the mountain. But we have to go now, and you'll need to hide until then."

"The kitchen staff is going to come and make lunch soon," Christoff said. "Hide in the back behind that shelf until we come for you."

"Thank you!" Basil said. He beamed again. "I'll prepare a poem for the occasion."

"Hey, Basil," said Naomi, before they closed the freezer door, "How did we even find your family? It didn't make any sense. We walked through some kind of strange tunnel of snow that felt like—like magic, somehow. And then we were suddenly somewhere else with your family."

"Oh, yes," said Basil, shrugging. "Yetis aren't found unless we want to be. We live on the peak of the mountain, but we've created several magical routes that lead us right into the human areas." He scratched his head thoughtfully. "They must have been so upset that they forgot to close one of the tunnels."

Chills crawled up Soraya's spine. "I didn't know yetis could make *magic tunnels*."

Basil lifted his furry chin. "Poetry is better than magic tunnels," he declared.

Christoff ran over to a counter, picked up a basket of fruit, and brought it into the freezer. "Here you go, Basil. We've got to go now, but I know you must be hungry."

"Oh my goodness, another feast!" Basil said, stuffing a pear into his mouth.

Soraya couldn't help it. "Can I give you a hug?" she asked Basil. "It's a human thing to show that you care about someone."

Basil nodded, and a delighted smile came over his face as he hugged her back. "Can I hug all humans?" he asked.

"I wouldn't lead with that, buddy," said Christoff. "I mean, you can hug us, but for everyone else, maybe a handshake first?"

Basil looked down at his enormous claws.

"We'll be back soon. *Remember to hide if anyone besides us comes in here.*"

"Okay."

They left Basil happily munching a mango and closed the freezer door.

"*Now* what?" whispered Naomi. "We have to sneak back into the dining room somehow."

"Yeah," said Christoff, gulping. "And the kitchen staff is going to serve lunch soon, which means they might look in the freezer. So whatever we're going to do, we had better do it fast."

Punished

"Where have you three *been*?" demanded Soraya's mom when Soraya, Naomi, and Christoff straggled back into the dining room to join the rest of the class. "What were you *doing*?"

"They were prowling around upstairs," announced the Animal Control worker triumphantly. He had beaten them downstairs and appeared to be in the process of telling on them.

"I was sick," said Christoff. He turned and gave a not-very-convincing cough. "And I was too embarrassed to get sick in here. So I, uh, went to my room. But then I accidentally puked on my sheets and I had to throw them in the laundry."

Even Soraya had to admit it was not a very believable story. Her mother glared daggers at them, but just then a shout came from outside the dining room doors.

"All finished!" Another Animal Control worker pushed her way into the room. "We've searched the lodge from top to bottom, and we can confirm there are no wild animals of any kind inside the building." She winked at Ms. Staples. "It looks like whatever it was has left."

Soraya could tell the woman didn't believe there really had been an animal in the lodge, which was a relief. It was safer for Basil if everyone assumed that Abby had just imagined something.

"I swear I saw a monster!" Abby cried from across the room.

"All right, everyone—back to normal," called out Mr. Haroyan. "Put away your parkas and return your ski equipment, please."

"The lodge staff can get back to work now," said a harried-looking Ms. Wilber. "We'll serve lunch in about an hour."

Soraya, Christoff, and Naomi glanced at each other. Everyone else mumbled and muttered quietly, still speculating about whether Abby had seen anything. A small crowd of kids gathered around Abby, asking her questions.

"Please stop harassing Abby," said Ms. Staples. "Out of your parkas, everyone."

Soraya's mom turned to Soraya and her friends again. "It was *incredibly* irresponsible of you kids to wander off when we all thought there was a wild animal on the loose."

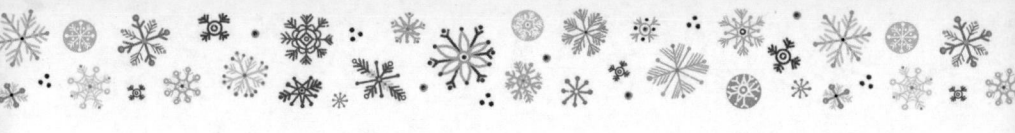

"Ms. Kadar!" called Eli. He ran up to Soraya's mom and tugged at her hand. "Ms. Kadar, since we lost some rehearsal time today, can we rehearse a little before lunch? I don't know all my lines yet."

"What? Oh, yes—the play," said Soraya's mom. She blinked like she'd just remembered there was a play. Then she looked back at Soraya, Christoff, and Naomi. "I'm not done with you three."

"I told you, Mom, Abby's eyesight isn't that great," said Soraya.

Her mom sighed. "That's not the point. I have to go help with the play, but we'll be having a conversation later, Soraya."

Trying to look as sorry as possible, the three of them hung their heads and slowly trudged out of the dining room. As soon as they were in the hall, though, they raced up the steps to the third floor, where they retrieved their coats and boots from under the chair.

"They're about to *start cooking in the kitchen*," said Soraya. "If people go into the freezer, do you think Basil can stay hidden?"

"If no one goes to the very back, he might be okay," said Christoff, biting his lip. "*Might* be. If he can hide behind, say, a thousand pounds of meat. Maybe they'll think he's just a big, hairy pillar of frost."

"We have to hope so because we can't go check on him right now," said Naomi. "We're in enough trouble already."

They headed back to the lobby to sit around the fire before lunch. Naomi chose their seats strategically. "Let's sit where your mom can see us being good and quiet," she said.

The lodge had resumed normal activity. Everyone was forbidden to tease Abby, who had curled into a corner with a book. Every once in a while, she looked up and glanced around at everyone suspiciously. Other students were clustered in groups, talking and laughing.

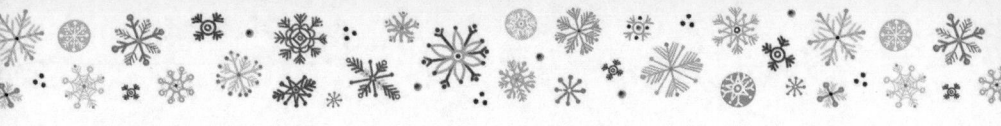

While Christoff and Naomi played chess, Soraya pulled out her sketchbook and worked on drawings for her comic book by the fire. The time flew by, like it always did when she was thinking up worlds.

Her mom bustled in and out of the dining room, carrying props for the play. There were festive-looking strings of lights, bags of cotton balls to make fake snow, and even a garland from a decorated tree in the lobby left over from Christmas.

"Why don't you rehearse your lines while I get the props together?" Ms. Kadar said to Lance as he trailed behind her. "Remember, the Snow Queen is a *villain*..."

Soraya caught a glimpse of her mom's face. It was bright and open, and her eyes shone. Soraya couldn't stop staring.

"What's wrong?" said Christoff.

"My mom's just *really* into this play. She's actually excited about it. It's *weird*."

"That's good. Maybe it'll help her forget that she was mad at us a few minutes ago."

"I just wish we could check on Basil," said Naomi. "He must be terrified down there."

All through lunch, the three of them ate nervously, expecting to hear a deafening shriek coming from the kitchen. But that didn't happen, to Soraya's great relief.

"Listen up, everyone," Soraya's mom said, standing up. Soraya almost choked on a mouthful of her sandwich. "Those of you in the play will join me in rehearsing this afternoon. Remember, we are going to put on our dress rehearsal during dinner tonight, so I hope everyone will join us."

Everyone cheered. Soraya peeked at Naomi and Christoff. She knew they were all thinking the same thing: this afternoon would be a perfect time to bring Basil back to his family, while her mom was busy with the play.

But Soraya's mom leaned across the table to Soraya. "I want you kids to stay nearby and in my sight, all right? You can do whatever you want out in the lobby, but if you're not in here or with one of your teachers, I want you where I can see you."

"Mom, we're not five years old!" Soraya protested.

"When you go wandering off while there's a wild animal supposedly on the loose, it makes me question your judgment, Soraya," her mom said. "Besides, you still get to do what you want. I just want an adult near you."

"*Mom...*"

"Can you give us a minute?" her mom asked Christoff and Naomi.

They both nodded and looked only too happy to escape the table.

Soraya's mom sat down next to her. Soraya thought fast. There was only one option left: be as sorry as possible.

She hung her head and tried to look humble. "I'm really sorry, Mom. I didn't believe Abby, but I can see now why that was wrong."

Soraya's mom looked surprised. "Well...I'm glad you see that your judgment could have been better. Abby might not have the best eyesight, but that doesn't mean she didn't see something."

Soraya tried to look pitiful. "You're right."

Her mom squinted at her. "Are you feeling okay, Soraya?"

"Yeah. I'm just thinking about how I can do better next time."

Still looking suspicious, her mom said, "Well, I have to say I'm really glad that you, Christoff, and Naomi have become so close. It's good to see you with friends."

Soraya nodded, surprised. She hadn't expected her mom to say anything nice... although she had been on a campaign for years to try to get Soraya to make friends.

"What did you kids do the rest of the morning?" her mom asked. "I saw you by the fire. Anything interesting?"

"Not really," Soraya said quickly. "You know, just—reading."

"Okay," her mom said slowly. "I just thought—"

"I need to go to the bathroom, Mom. Sorry."

"All right," said her mom, standing up. She looked a little sad. "I hope you enjoy the play tonight."

Soraya looked up. "Do we have to go? It's only the dress rehearsal, right?"

"Oh—well, I was hoping you'd come. Everyone has worked so hard…"

Soraya was about to protest, but something stopped her. She hadn't seen her mom look quite this sad in a long time, not since her dad had left. Usually her mom acted like everything was fine.

"Okay, Mom," Soraya heard herself say. "We'll come to the play."

Her mom smiled. "Thank you. I know it might not be your cup of tea, but I really appreciate it. Once you get back from the bathroom, remember to stay where I can see you for the afternoon."

Soraya slumped. "Okay," she said. Her plan hadn't worked. She hurried out to the lobby, and plopped down next to her friends. "It's no use. We have to stay close by. So unfair."

"That's better than what my mom would've done," said Christoff. "I would have been grounded for a month."

"We'll have to take Basil back tonight," said Naomi. "He can't just live in the freezer."

The day wore on. Soraya managed to complete several pages of her new ice planet comic. In her humble opinion, it was *almost* as good as a Nimbla Moony comic. Almost.

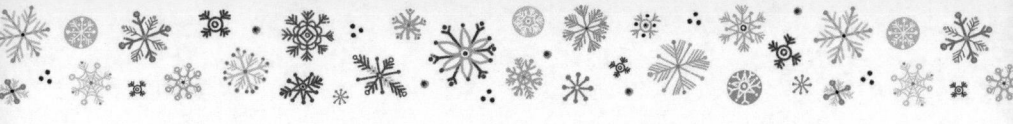

She glanced up every few minutes to make sure her mom was nowhere close by, but her mom was safely in the dining hall, setting up the stage for the rehearsal.

"It looks pretty cool in there," Christoff said after getting up to peek through the doors. "Your mom did a really good job with the decorating. The play is going to start in about half an hour."

Just then, Naomi rushed toward them, her eyes wide and terrified.

"Come here *right now*, both of you," she said. "Hurry."

The Last-Minute Prop

Naomi turned on her heel and strode across the lobby toward the coat closet near the front door. Soraya stuffed her sketchbook under her shirt as she followed; she couldn't risk leaving it on the chair.

"Come on," said Naomi in a high voice, pulling Christoff and Soraya inside the large walk-in closet. It appeared to be empty, other than a long row of coats and hangers.

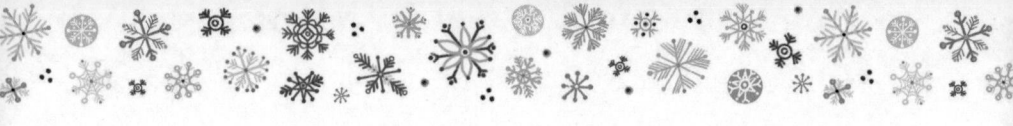

Naomi flipped on a light. Then she walked to the very end of the closet and pulled aside some coats.

Soraya peered behind them and gasped.

There was Basil, huddled in the corner. The yeti's eyes were half-closed and he looked sick again.

"What are you doing here?" Soraya whispered. "We told you to stay in the freezer!"

"I heard some people say they were going to clean out the freezer," said Basil weakly. "And you said no humans should see me, and they would have seen me. So I sneaked away and tried to hide. When I saw that human—" He pointed at Naomi. "I knew she was a safe human, so I called out to her—"

"I caught him wandering down this hall," Naomi said breathlessly. "Thank *goodness* no one else saw him first."

"Basil, we're not supposed to leave Soraya's mom's sight right now," said Christoff. "Otherwise, we could just take you home."

"Not really," said Naomi. "There are still people all over the grounds and skiers riding on the lift. People would see him if he went out now."

"He's going to get sick again," Soraya said, feeling his forehead. "We have to figure out what to do with him until the play is over."

She thought as fast as she could. A possibly-very-bad-idea started to form.

"Hey," she said slowly, "there was an old cooler in the attic, right? And there's an ice machine in our hallway."

"Yeah?" said Christoff, his eyebrows raised.

"I have an idea," said Soraya. The others just stared at her as she began to explain her plan to them.

"It's pretty crazy," said Naomi when Soraya had finished.

"It might be our only option to keep Basil safe," said Christoff.

"Okay," said Naomi. "But if this is going to work, one of us should stay out in the lobby by the fire the whole time, just so that if Soraya's mom looks out she'll think two of us have just gone to the bathroom or something. Also—whoever stays in the lobby can gather some, um, materials."

They divvied up the duties for Soraya's plan, and took off.

Ten minutes later, Christoff and Soraya met back up in the closet. Christoff was dragging a huge rolling cooler. Soraya lugged two bags of ice.

"What's happening?" said Basil weakly, as Soraya dumped the ice into the cooler.

"Basil," said Soraya breathlessly, "have you ever heard of a play?"

"Is a play a thing that humans do?"

"It's like pretending while an audience watches. Come on, get in."

She reached down and helped Basil step into the ice-filled cooler. Right away, his eyes cleared a little.

"Stay here a second. I have to get something."

She dashed out to the lobby, where Naomi quickly handed her a bag.

"I gathered all the decorations you asked for from the lobby," Naomi whispered. "But I just thought of something. We need to find a way to distract Abby and keep her out here in the lobby, so she doesn't accidentally see Basil and recognize him. So I'll stay out here while you two go and watch the play."

"Good idea." Soraya raced back to the closet. She closed the door behind her and dumped out the contents of the bag.

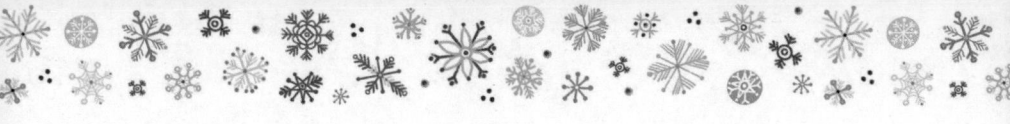

"Basil, you're going to be a prop in the play," Christoff said. "Being a prop is the *most important part*."

"Remember how you said yetis can stand very still to camouflage themselves?" said Soraya. "You'll have to do that now. It's only for an hour, and then once it's dark outside we can take you home."

Basil blinked as Soraya wrapped a Christmas tree skirt around his waist. She made sure it covered the ice and the cooler and then slung a green garland around him.

"What is my part in the play?" Basil asked excitedly. "What kind of prop am I?" Evidently Christoff had been explaining theater to him.

"You're the most important creature in the woods," Soraya said. "But remember, Basil, you can't move."

Basil did a great job of freezing his smile in place and not moving a muscle as Soraya and Christoff wheeled the cooler out of the closet and toward the dining hall. Soraya's heart ker-thumped in her chest; she was almost dizzy with fear.

They wheeled Basil all the way into the dining hall. Only someone looking closely would have noticed the fear and awe in his eyes at seeing so many people. To his credit, he didn't move.

"Hey, Mom," Soraya called, her voice tight with terror.

Her mom turned to her.

"I felt bad about earlier, so I decided to contribute to the play," said Soraya. "We found this yeti stuffed animal in the attic. I thought it could be part of the scenery."

Her mom's face softened. "Well, it's very realistic. This is lovely of you, Soraya."

"Thanks, Mom. Do you mind if we place it on the stage, just so I can feel like I added a touch of my own?"

"Sure, honey. Just make sure it's far back, so we have enough space. Maybe you could put it between the snowy hills."

"Thanks, Mom!" Soraya's knees nearly buckled with relief.

The curtains were already down in front of the stage. Soraya and Christoff went to the left of the stage, and wheeled Basil up a ramp that led to the wings and onto the stage.

"Okay, Basil," said Christoff, who looked as nervous as Soraya felt. "We're sticking you right back here. You'll be a beautiful snow-poet for all to see."

Basil beamed, but he was already taking direction very well; he didn't say a thing.

After they secured Basil between two large painted cardboard "snowy hills" and a pile of fake snow, Soraya and Christoff went to sit down with the rest of the audience, near the front.

All around them, other guests and students filled the dining hall, smiling appreciatively. Soraya saw her mom standing in the wings helping the costumed kids get ready to go on stage.

Soraya's foot jiggled; the play couldn't be over fast enough for her.

Ms. Staples climbed onto the stage and took the microphone. "May I have your attention! It's time for our dress rehearsal of *The Snow Queen*. First, thank you to Alpine Lodge for giving us this opportunity. They've been so gracious. Please enjoy!"

The curtains slowly rose. Soraya gulped at the sight of Basil standing stock-still in

his cooler of ice with a garland draped over him. But he didn't move, and he didn't look especially noticeable among the rest of the props on the set, which was what she had hoped for.

The first person to speak was Derek, who played Kai. He walked out onto the stage and declared, "What a winter wonderworld, Gerta! Isn't it beautiful?"

Meili was playing Gerta. She stepped out onto the stage next. "Yes, Kai! It's lovely out here. Let's play!"

Soraya watched with interest despite herself. She liked *watching* plays, she just didn't enjoy being in them.

When it came time for the Snow Queen's appearance, Noor, who played the queen, came out onstage dressed in an elegant, queenly costume sprinkled with fake snow.

Noor gazed out at the audience and froze.

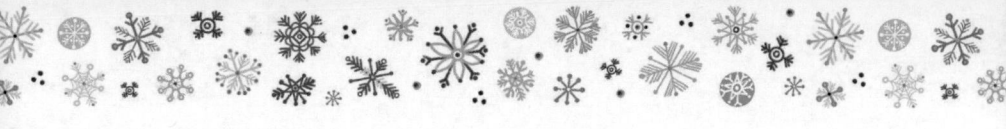

"Noor," Soraya's mom whispered to her. "Your line is, 'Hello, young man. Are you lost?'"

Noor stared for another second.

Then she burst into tears, sobbed, "I can't do this," and raced off the stage.

The audience murmured, but sat politely. It was obvious that people felt sorry for Noor. But Soraya watched her mom, who was standing just offstage. Her face had an expression Soraya had never seen before. She turned red, her eyes were bright, and her lips were pursed. She looked like she was trying to decide something.

Then she squared her shoulders and stepped out onto the stage.

Soraya expected her mom to tell everyone the rehearsal was canceled or delayed.

Instead, what came out of her mother's mouth was, "Hello, young man. Are you lost?"

Soraya almost fell off her chair. Her mom was saying the Snow Queen's lines!

Derek did a double take, then seemed to realize what was going on. "I'm just very cold," he replied, which was his next line.

"That's only natural. It is, after all, my kingdom you've entered," said Ms. Kadar. Her voice was powerful and regal like a real queen's. She held herself straight and poised.

Next to Soraya, Christoff's jaws dropped.

The audience was silent for a moment, then burst out in applause. Even Derek cheered, forgetting to stay in character for a second.

Soraya's mom flushed briefly, but she went on in that majestic voice that filled the dining hall, "Now tell me what it is you're looking for. There may be some way I can help."

Soraya truly felt as if she'd been hit by a truck. Not only was her mom saying the Snow Queen's lines, she was saying them *well*. She was saying them in a way that made the audience *feel* things.

"Whoa," said Christoff.

The play went on. Soraya could tell the kids were happy to be saying their lines with her mom. What was more, her mom seemed happy, too—she was almost glowing.

"I can't *believe* it," Soraya whispered.

She was so mesmerized that she made it almost all the way to the end of the play before she thought to look at Basil. When she did notice him, she stiffened in her seat: Basil's eyes were half-closed. He was looking droopier by the second.

She hissed to get Christoff's attention. "The stage lights," she said. "I forgot how hot they would be for him."

"What if he faints?" whispered Christoff.

"He only has to make it a few more minutes," Soraya said, biting her lip. "Can you slip out quickly and tell Naomi to get our coats ready? As soon as the show is over, one of us should distract my mom and someone else should grab Basil."

Christoff tiptoed out into the lobby to give Naomi the message. "You should be the one to distract your mom. I'll get Basil and try to roll him to the back door," he said to Soraya when he returned. "We'll meet you outside. I'm sure your mom will want to hear what you thought of the play."

Soraya nodded, wringing her hands. She sat at the edge of her seat until the show was over and the dining room exploded into applause.

Everyone stood up to clap when the curtain went down and all the actors stood in front of it, bowing.

Christoff seized the opportunity to sneak around the stage to the back. Soraya saw him hurry behind the curtain, and a minute later he wheeled Basil down the ramp.

"Mom!" Soraya called, so her mom wouldn't turn around.

Her mom beamed and looked a little embarrassed at all the people cheering for her.

"Hi, honey," her mom said, bending toward her. "I hope that wasn't too much. I didn't mean to step in for Noor—it's just that everyone else needed to rehearse, and I knew that no one else knew her lines—"

"What are you *talking* about, Mom? You were amazing!" said Soraya. She studied her mom's face. "Mom, where did you learn to do that? You never told me you could act."

"Oh..." Her mom grew flustered. Then she met Soraya's eyes, and her own eyes looked a little wet. "It's a long story."

"Do you promise you'll tell me about it later?" Soraya said.

Her mom fidgeted with her hands, then sighed. "I—all right. I promise."

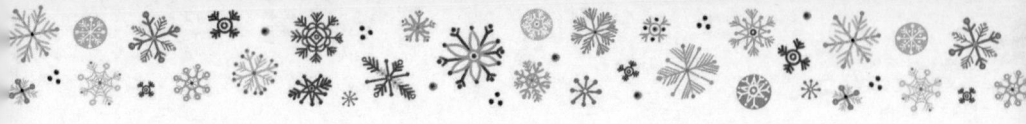

"Ms. Kadar! Ms. Kadar! Did I say my lines right?" asked Eli.

"You did great, Eli," Soraya's mom said. "We'll go over it in a minute. I'm going to go talk to Noor first and make sure she is all right."

Grateful for the timing, Soraya slipped out of the dining hall.

Now all she and her friends had to do was somehow sneak out of the lodge unseen, find a magic passage to the top of the mountain, and support Basil—without getting eaten by a troop of terrifying yetis.

She hurried off.

A Poet's Request

Soraya speed-walked toward the front door, looking around as she moved through the lobby to make sure no one was watching. Naomi was gesturing at her frantically. She was already at the door, standing next to a cooler full of water and bits of melting ice.

She handed Soraya her snow boots and parka. "Get them on, quick," she said. "We'll meet you outside."

Soraya slipped on her coat and boots in record time. In front of the lodge, she found Christoff, Naomi, and Basil—who looked much healthier again—huddled behind a large planter near the front doors.

"You were perfect in the play, Basil!" said Soraya, patting his shoulder.

He beamed. "I tried my best to be a good prop," he said. "I stayed still even when I felt like I was burning up."

"Well, now that we are taking you back to your family, you won't be burning up anymore," she assured him.

"Soraya, Christoff," said Naomi. "How are we going to get Basil to the top of the mountain? The ski lift doesn't operate this late. Plus, don't we have to find one of those yeti tunnels to reach his family?"

"I can open a tunnel," suggested Basil.

"Like that magic tunnel we found before?" cried Christoff. "You know how to do that?"

Basil shrugged. "All yetis know how to do that. Otherwise we'd be seen all the time."

"Whoa!" said Soraya. "That is *so* cool." She glanced back at the door. "You should hurry and do it, Basil, before someone comes out here and sees us."

Basil stood very still and spread his shaggy arms out in front of him. And then, to Soraya's wonderment, a tunnel formed before their eyes: swirling flakes that stretched ahead of them, making a passage.

Basil lowered his arms. His expression was nervous all of a sudden.

"Come on," he said, hanging his head. He took Soraya's hand. "Might as well go."

Soraya gulped. "We'll be right there, Basil, if you need us."

The four of them walked into the tunnel. That indescribable feeling of magic flooded Soraya again. This time, as they hiked through, the tunnel closed up behind them until she couldn't see the snowy field in front of the lodge anymore.

Christoff and Naomi stayed glued to her side. As they neared the end of the tunnel, wild roars echoed up ahead.

Basil gripped Soraya's hand. "They sound pretty mad. I hope they like my poem."

"We'll help if we need to, Basil," she assured him, avoiding the murderous looks she knew Naomi and Christoff were giving her.

They neared the same cliff face they'd seen before. Below the cliff ran a narrow ledge. Basil pointed at it and turned to them.

"You can stay down here," he said.

Soraya nodded. She was more than happy to stay hidden. "Remember how brave you are, and that you're a great poet. You can do this."

She slipped down onto the ledge along with Christoff and Naomi.

Basil looked terrified, but he stood up straight and marched toward his family.

"Excuse me!" he called out. "Mother, Father, Grandfather, Grandmother. Aunts, uncles, cousins. Family. I've come back! But I need to tell you something."

Instantly, the wails stopped, leaving a stunned silence.

Soraya gripped the side of the cliff.

Then she heard a sound that could only be described as a wild whooping.

"Basil, darling!" cried a yeti.

Soraya, Christoff, and Naomi stood on their tiptoes to peek above the ledge. Basil stood in the middle of his shocked family. He truly was tiny compared to them.

"I knew you'd come back," cried another yeti. "I knew it!"

Basil turned to the biggest yeti, who must have been 14 feet tall. "Hi, Grandma," he said.

"We were so worried," said the grandmother yeti in a booming voice. "What were you thinking, wandering off?"

Basil tried to square his quivering shoulders. "I needed some time away," he said.

"Time away from your home?" said another yeti. "But this is where you belong!"

Basil squared his shoulders more firmly. "I'm not so sure about that," he said.

The yetis gasped, which sounded like the wind being sucked backwards.

"You don't mean that, Basil," said one of the older yetis.

"I do." Basil planted his feet. "I'm not the yeti you want me to be."

They gasped again.

"I don't *want* to scare people. I'm—I'm a pacifist."

One of the yetis gave a shocked yelp. "A *what*?" he said, as if Basil had just claimed he was an octopus.

"A pacifist. I like peaceful things, and I don't want to scare people. I don't even like to eat meat. I'm a vegetarian."

Another one of the yetis fainted and tumbled to the ground, causing the whole mountain to quake.

A third yeti started wailing again. "*Peaceful* things? How are you going to keep up yeti traditions if you like *peaceful* things?"

"That's just it," said Basil. "I don't want to keep up yeti traditions. I want to write poetry."

"Basil, you can't be serious," said his mother. "Have we raised you wrong? Is that why you don't want to scare people?"

"No," said Basil. "I just love poetry, that's all. I'm quite good at it, too. Would you like to hear a poem?"

"A what?" said Basil's grandmother, who seemed hard of hearing.

"A poem. I wrote it myself." Basil cleared his throat and stood taller as he recited his poem.

> *A big iceberg floats*
> *Across the sea and I feel*
> *The iceberg is me.*

Basil took a low bow. When he straightened up again, he was flushed but looked proud.

"What was that?" said the mother yeti. "Are you reading a map?"

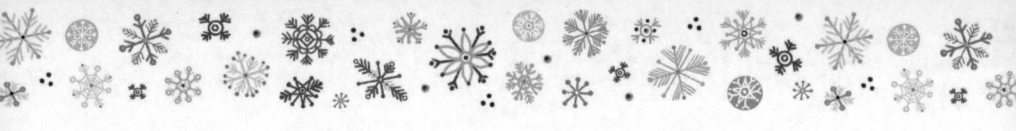

"No. *That*," said Basil, "was a poem. A haiku, actually." He puffed out his chest.

"Ridiculous!" said his grandmother, her voice so loud that the trees shook. "For centuries, we've—"

"I know," said Basil, shaking his head. "We've scared people."

"It's what we've always done," said another one of the older yetis.

"But it's not what we have to *keep* doing, Grandpa," said Basil. "There's no yeti law that says that's what we have to do. Why don't we make people feel *good*?"

The yetis looked around at each other as if Basil had just suggested that they try swallowing fire.

"We should try it," Basil said. "I'll teach you all how to write poetry. Go on, Grandpa. Describe the rock you're sitting on, but do it in a creative way."

Basil's grandfather knit his brows. "The rock is quite...big. It is chunky. It is gray. It is under me."

"Fantastic!" cried Basil, clapping. "See, that's a poem!"

His grandfather didn't look convinced.

But just then another yeti burst out, "I don't know why that poem makes me cry, but it does! It's so beautiful—I never realized how special rocks are."

He dissolved into sobs.

"See?" said Basil. "Poetry is powerful. I'd rather write poetry than do anything else." He lifted his chin. "And I'm not going to scare people anymore. My talents lie elsewhere."

"Oh, Basil, you were always such a dreamer," said his mother tearfully. She grabbed the hand of another giant yeti who must have been Basil's father.

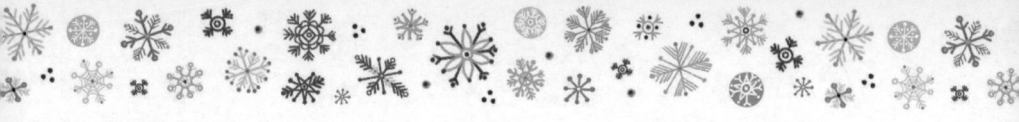

"Promise me you won't make me scare people if I stay here," said Basil. His voice shook, but his feet were still planted firmly. "If you make me scare people, I'm leaving again. And this time it will be for good."

Soraya wondered if Basil's family could see him trembling.

The other yetis gasped. The one who had fainted sat up, heard what Basil said, and then fainted again.

"I want you to let me be who I really am," Basil went on. "And I don't want you to make fun of me, or make me feel weird for doing what I love."

Basil's father cleared his throat. "We promise, Basil. We're glad to have you back, son. You and your poetry."

Basil looked shocked. "Thank you, Papa! Hey...there's another thing I learned that I want to show you." He ran over to his father

and threw his arms around him. "It's called a hug. Isn't it marvelous?"

Basil's father hugged him back clumsily, his huge arms nearly knocking the little yeti to the ground.

"I want to try it," said Basil's mother, stomping her way over to them. She wrapped her arms around Basil so tightly he wheezed. "Okay, that's enough, Mom," he said.

After Basil had hugged every member of his family, he said, "Give me just a second."

"Where are you going?" cried his mother as he walked away.

"I'll be right back. I promise."

Basil hurried over and climbed down onto the ledge, beaming. "They're going to let me write poetry!" he exclaimed.

"I know!" Soraya hugged him, hard. "You were really brave, Basil."

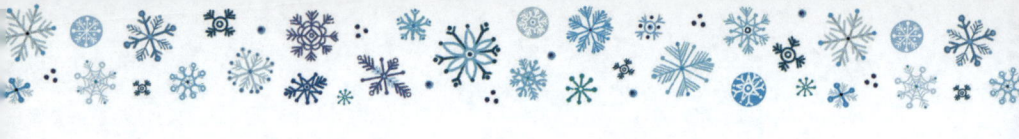

He lifted his head high. "I was, wasn't I?"

"You were great, Basil," Christoff said.

"Will you come and see me again?" asked Basil. "By then I'll have a whole book of poetry."

"Of course we will. And speaking of poetry, I have a present for you," said Soraya. She fished inside her parka and pulled out a blank

spiral notebook. "This is so you can write down all your poems. There's a pen clipped on there too."

Basil clutched the notebook to his chest. Tears filled his eyes. "For me?"

"Yup." Soraya smiled sadly. "We'll miss you, Basil. But we need to get back now before the teachers send out a search party."

"Oh. Yes, of course." He spread out his arms again, and there it was—another tunnel, leading right back to the lawn in front of the lodge. "Promise you won't forget me?"

"How could we forget you?" said Naomi. "Basil, the soon-to-be world-famous poet."

"That's right," said Soraya. "Plus, I'm already planning the comic I'll write about you." Soraya hugged him again, and then the three friends plunged into the magic tunnel.

This time, they ran. In just a few seconds, they were back on the grounds of the lodge.

Soraya turned around to look back at Basil, but the tunnel had closed up behind Christoff and Naomi.

"He's really gone," she said. Her chest ached.

"No, he's up there," Christoff said, pointing at the mountain. "We know where to find him, at least."

"Come on, let's get back in case anyone is looking for us," said Naomi. "I can only imagine what will happen if they realize we're missing a second time."

A Confession

To Soraya's relief, no one noticed them slip back inside the lodge. The lobby was filled with students sitting around, chatting, drinking hot chocolate, and playing board games. Mr. Haroyan sat in a comfy chair, looking relaxed for the first time on the whole trip. Other students and Ms. Staples were gathered near the door, wearing their parkas and pulling on their boots.

Soraya, Naomi, and Christoff hurried out of sight, pulled off their coats and boots, and went back into the lobby.

"I should go talk to my mom," Soraya said.

"Sure," said Naomi. She patted Soraya's shoulder. "Good luck."

Soraya put her parka on a chair by the fire. She swallowed; her friends didn't even know exactly what she planned to do.

She steeled herself. If Basil could do it, she could do it too.

She walked slowly toward the dining hall, where a few people were cleaning up tables. Students and parent chaperones were helping clean up the stage.

She walked up to her mom, who was sweeping some glitter into a pile.

"Mom?"

Her mom turned. "Oh—hi, honey."

"Can we talk for a minute?"

Her mom looked surprised. Soraya had never in her life requested to have a talk.

"Right now?"

"Yeah."

"Uh, sure." Her mom put down the broom and followed Soraya to one of the empty tables in the back corner.

"Okay, Mom," Soraya said. "First tell me how you were so good as the Snow Queen."

For a fleeting second, Soraya saw the strangest look on her mom's face—like she was afraid of getting caught.

"How come you can act and you never told me?" Soraya asked.

Her mom fidgeted with her hands and then let out a heavy sigh. "I suppose I should tell you a few things, Soraya." She dropped her voice. "I—I used to do some acting. When I was younger."

"You *did*? But you're an accountant!" Soraya stared. Her mom might as well have said she was from Mars. She couldn't wrap her head around it. Her normal, beige mom—an *actress*? "Where? When?"

Her moms' cheeks flamed. "Well, when I was younger, I was really involved with theater. I acted in school plays and in community theater shows."

Soraya's mouth dropped open again.

"But my parents—your grandparents—didn't approve." Now her mom was talking fast, like she was trying to squeeze the words out. She wiped her eyes. "They wanted me to do something more sensible."

"Like accounting?" said Soraya.

"Yes. Like accounting." She looked up at Soraya and tried to smile. "I was just a little older than you when everything changed. I was going to a theater school at the time, and I had so many friends there." Her face fell as she continued her story. "But your grandparents took me out of that school and put me in a school they thought was better for academics. I wasn't allowed to do theater anymore, and I lost all my friends."

"Mom, that *stinks*," said Soraya.

Her mom tried to smile again. "I know maybe I should have told you about some of this before…but I just didn't think it was important."

"How could you not think it was important?" Soraya cried. "Mom, you're a great actress!"

Her mom blushed. "That's a bit of an exaggeration."

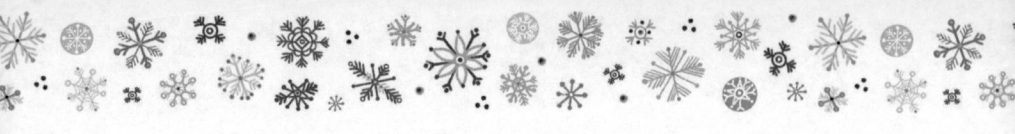

"It's not. You should start acting again," Soraya said.

"When you were really young, I got a few parts in local community theater plays," her mom said in a small voice. "But your dad didn't like me spending time away from home." She looked down. "I wish sometimes that I had...well, that I had stood up for myself, and kept acting anyway." She looked back up and shrugged. "But that's neither here nor there, now."

A familiar brick settled in Soraya's stomach.

"Was that my fault, too?" she whispered.

"Was what your fault?" asked her mom.

"Did you stop acting because of me, too?" Soraya braced herself for the answer.

Her mom's jaw dropped in shock. "Of *course* that wasn't your fault. You were a tiny little girl!" She studied Soraya. "Why would you think that was *your* fault?"

"It just seems like...Dad left us because I'm so weird."

Her mom gave Soraya a strange look. "Honey, your father didn't leave because he thought you were weird."

"But he *did*," Soraya said, tears rushing to her eyes. "He always acted like I was weird."

Her mom looked stunned for a second. Then she pulled Soraya in for a hug. "Your father left because of differences between the two of us, not because of you. At all."

Soraya sniffled. She hadn't planned on crying, and she was annoyed at herself. "But he never calls. He doesn't even write. It must be because of me."

"I don't know why he doesn't call, Soraya. But it doesn't have anything to do with you." Her mom paused. "I know that it's not fair to you that he doesn't call, and that it makes you sad."

Soraya pulled back. Something unhitched itself in her gut. Just a little bit, but she could feel it.

She studied her mom. Usually she didn't feel like her mom truly listened to her. But she could tell that right at that moment, she was listening. Her mom also looked a bit scared.

"You were a great Snow Queen, Mom," Soraya said. "Seriously." She thought of Basil's courage up on the mountain when he had stood up to his whole family. She drew herself up taller, tried to calm her nerves, and said, "I have a confession, too."

"What's that?" Her mom dabbed her eyes with a tissue.

"I want to be a comic book artist." Before her mom could say anything, she barreled ahead, "It's the only thing I want to do. I love comic books. I've already written and drawn a few. And I don't want to hide them from you anymore." She thought again of Basil's courage. "I want you to support me."

She sat stiffly while her mom stared at her. It was a different look than she'd ever seen on her mom's face.

"Just because your parents didn't let you do what you want, that doesn't mean you have to do the same thing to me," Soraya added. "There are lots of successful comic book artists. I'm going to be one of them."

Her mom waited a moment before she spoke. "Okay."

"*What?*" said Soraya. She was sure she had heard wrong.

"You're right," said her mom, and she actually laughed. "I don't want to do the same thing to you that my parents did to me." Then her face got more serious. "I guess I've been trying to protect you, but I haven't done it the right way." She brightened. "When you get older, we'll come up with a business plan. We'll have to make sure you have a good income with it. And—"

"*Mom*, I'm ten. We have time." Soraya felt strange—bewildered, happy, and lighter than she ever had. "Can—can I show you something?"

Her mom smiled. "Sure."

"Hold on," said Soraya. "I'll be right back." She flew out of the dining room, grabbed her sketchbook from the lobby, and raced back to her mom.

"Look," she said, thrusting her comics down onto the table between them. "This is one I made about Estelle the mermaid, and I made this one about Humphrey the dragon."

Soraya's heart thumped as she waited for her mom's reaction. Her mom flipped slowly through the pages, smiling.

"These are wonderful, honey," she said. A tear slipped down her face. "You're very talented."

"Jeez, mom, they're not supposed to make you cry." Soraya hugged her mom. "You really like them?"

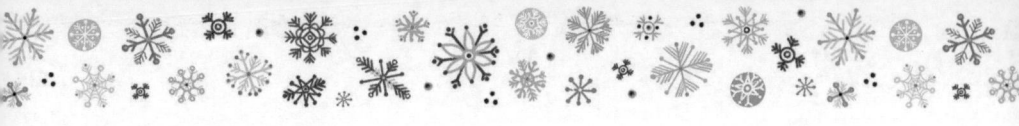

"I do like them." Her mom sniffled. "They're very creative."

Soraya felt like she was walking on air. She had never imagined she could ever feel this happy.

"Ms. Kadar, where do you want us to put the fake snow?" someone called from the stage.

"Oh, I should get back to helping them," her mom said. She hugged Soraya again. "I'm proud of you."

"You are?"

"Yes. And you will make many more amazing comic books, I know it."

Soraya held onto her comics as she watched her mom head back to the stage.

She walked back into the lobby, where she saw Christoff and Naomi sitting by the fire. They raised their eyebrows at her quizzically, like they were asking how the talk went.

Soraya held a finger up to her friends, letting them know she'd be there in a second. She had noticed Abby sitting in the corner alone again, curled over a book.

Soraya crossed the lobby to the corner. She bent down and whispered, "Hey, Abby."

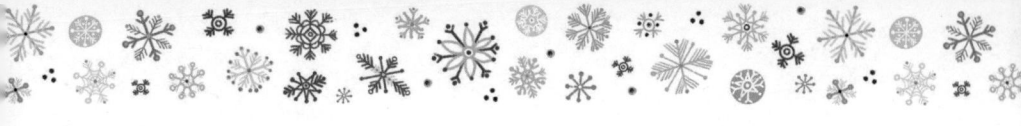

Abby looked up. "Yeah?"

"You weren't wrong. There really *was* a monster."

Abby dropped her book, sat straight up, and stared at Soraya.

"But it was a good monster," Soraya went on. "A yeti. A sweet young one. We rescued him. We had to hide him because other people would have hurt him if they found him."

"A yeti?" Abby held her breath.

"Yup," Soraya said. "I just wanted you to know that you weren't imagining things."

Abby's eyes shone. "I *knew* it," she said in a hushed voice. "I *knew* I saw something."

Soraya smiled and walked back over to the fire, where her friends were waiting for her.

Don't miss the other books in the Soraya series, *Soraya & the Mermaid* and *Soraya & the Dragon*. And coming in 2023, the magic adventures continue with *Soraya & the Loch Ness Monster*.

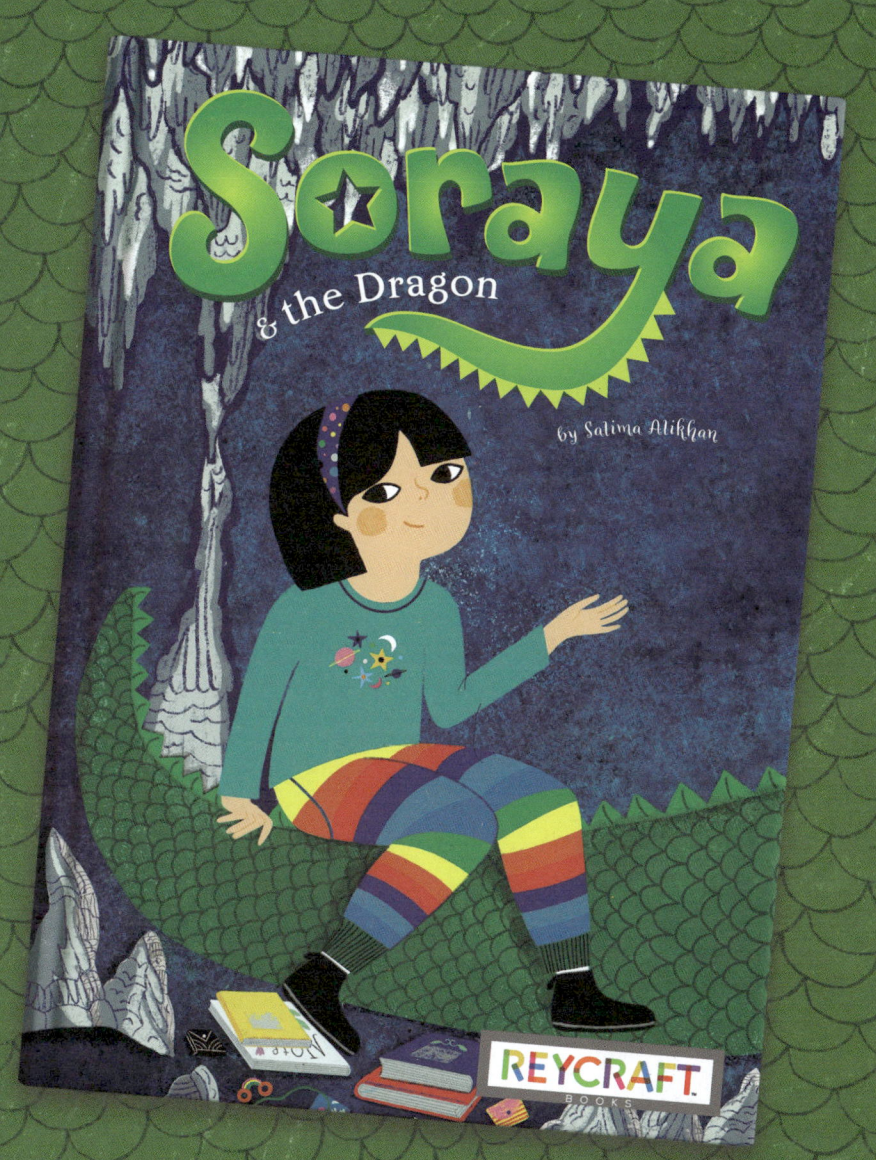

Salima Alikhan

has been a writer and illustrator for sixteen years. She lives in Austin, Texas, where she is also a college English and creative writing professor. When she went on school field trips as a child, she liked to imagine what sorts of creatures might be lurking in some of those fun places. She wrote stories and drew pictures about those creatures, and loves that she still gets to do that.

ILLUSTRATOR, *SORAYA & THE YETI*

Atieh Sohrabi

was born and raised in Tehran, Iran, and currently lives in New York City with her family. She started her career in industrial design before switching to a new path in illustrations. Her first illustrated book, published in 2002, received first prize in the 5th Tehran International Biennale Illustration. Since then, her books have appeared in exhibitions and museums around the world, winning numerous international awards.

ILLUSTRATOR, "BASIL GOES TO PANAMA"

Jennifer Naalchigar

is an illustrator based in Hertfordshire, England. She has a love for quirky characters and funny stories and enjoys experimenting with digital brushes. Jen can often be found doodling with her tablet in her local coffee shop. She also enjoys reading picture books to her daughter. She works in children's and educational publishing.